A PACKETFUL

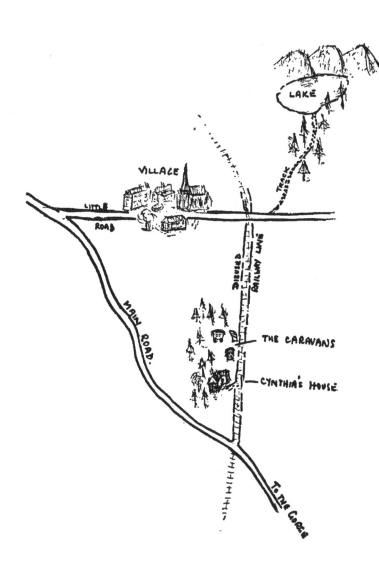

A PACKETFUL OF TROUBLE

by

MARGARET BACON

illustrated by

RICHARD TUCKWELL

HILL HOUSE PUBLICATIONS

By the same author

Going Down
The Episode
Kitty
The Unentitled
The Package
The Chain
Snow in Winter
The Kingdom of the Rose
The Serpent's Tooth

Travel
Journey to Guyana

Text copyright © 1974 by Margaret Bacon
Illustrations copyright Hill House Publications
All rights reserved
First published in Great Britain by
Dobson Books Ltd in 1974
First published in this edition by
Hill House Publications,
Highworth, Wiltshire SN6 7BZ

British Library Cataloguing in Publication Data
Bacon, Margaret
    Packetful of Trouble. – New ed
    I. Title   II. Tuckwell, Richard
    823.91 [J]

    ISBN 0–9513565–2–6

Cover illustration by Gary Samuel
Cover design by Jayne Brooks

Printed and bound in Great Britain by
Redwood Press Limited, Melksham, Wiltshire

CONTENTS

I

An Invitation

The Packet family lived near Dover. If they had not, this story would have been different. Probably it would not have happened at all.

This particular evening Rose Packet, who was ten, was sitting at one end of the table, painting. On the floor by her chair was a cardboard box. In it was her brown and white guinea pig, called Porky. Rose was having a lot of trouble with her picture; it was a seaside scene, but although the people and boats were all right, the sand did not look like sand and the sea was hopeless—it did not even look wet! It looked like a flat blue carpet.

Rose's brother Simon was sitting at the other end of the table doing his homework. He was only a year older than Rose but liked to think of himself as almost grown-up. He conducted experiments and built contraptions in the big untidy garden. He was pale and had black hair which stuck out round his head like starched wool. He wore spectacles with steel frames and did not mind that the boys at school nicknamed him The Professor. He had a tortoise called Fortescue and a pair of green stick insects which spent their time crawling about in a tall glass jar on the dresser.

Mr and Mrs Packet were sitting by the fire talking quietly.

'I had a letter from Cynthia this morning,' Mrs Packet was saying. 'She married a Frenchman, you know, and lives in the South of France. There's something in her letter which might solve our problem.'

Rose and Simon knew what the problem was. Their mother had just started a job, which was all right in term time, but the problem was what would happen to the children during the long school holidays.

'She has invited us all to go and stay there,' Mother explained.

Father looked alarmed. The idea of going away anywhere always horrified him. At least the idea of going anywhere except London, where he had a small printing business which he liked to go and visit whenever things got a bit difficult at home.

'I'll read you what she says,' Mother went on, taking a letter out of an envelope. 'Ah, here's the part I want. She writes: "It is lovely here. We are surrounded by pine forests

8

and hills. There is even a lake nearby. I'm sure you would love it. Why don't you all come and stay? In the field next to the garden we have two ancient caravans, a little field kitchen, and a tap. If you would like to borrow all these things we should be delighted to see you any time this summer . . ." '

'It's out of the question, of course,' Father interrupted.

'Well, yes,' Mother agreed. 'For me.'

'You're not suggesting that I should take the children? I can't—I'll be needed in London several times in August.'

Mother laughed. 'Don't worry,' she said. 'I was thinking that Rose and Simon might go. I mean if we could make some arrangement for somebody to take them there.'

Rose and Simon both stared at their parents.

'Oh, *please*, Dad,' Simon said, and his voice was very hoarse. 'You must let us go.'

Rose was gazing into space; she was imagining two little gypsy caravans in a meadow, she was dreaming of hills and pine forests.

'It would be ever so good for us,' Simon went on passionately. 'Think of the education of it. Now Rose learns French and . . .'

'Do you learn French?' Father asked her.

Rose came out of her dream.

'I don't know,' she said.

Simon glared at her. Sometimes he had a great desire to hit his sister: silly, dreamy thing.

He bent over her. 'Don't you see?' he hissed in her ear. 'We've got to make them want us to go.'

'But I don't think I do want to go,' Rose said in surprise. 'I mean, what about Porky?'

Simon looked with dislike at the plump brown and white form in the cardboard box. Porky looked up at him for a

9

moment but did not stop chewing the carrot which he was holding down with one paw. Somehow he managed to convey the impression that Simon was less important than a carrot.

'Look, Rose,' Simon said. 'I'd have to leave my stick insects, but I'm not fussing.'

'Oh, but they're different.'

'They're not. They're animals, just as much as guinea pigs are. They're jolly intelligent too and . . .'

'Yes, but they're not *cuddly*!'

'Oh, *girls*!' Simon said furiously and went out of the room, banging the door behind him.

Rose looked after him with mild surprise and then went back to her painting.

'You really must pack up now,' Mother told her. 'And put Porky back in the cage for the night.'

Rose cleared away her painting things and picked up Porky.

'I did just wonder,' Mrs Packet said to her husband, after Rose had gone out, 'if the cousins might be interested in going with Simon and Rose.'

'You mean Linda and James?'

Mother nodded.

The other Packets, their cousins, lived at the far side of the town. Felicity was still a toddler but Linda was the same age as Rose. James, the eldest, was fourteen.

'James is very capable,' Mother said. 'And I know he speaks good French. His mother said that he managed very well on that exchange last year; he stayed with a family in Paris, you know. The boys could have one caravan and the girls the other.'

'And Cynthia would keep an eye on them, you mean?' Father asked. He was getting quite keen on this holiday, now that he was sure that he would not be expected to go.

'Oh, I'm sure she would. It's just the travelling that's difficult.'

'You could discuss it with Claire,' Father said. Claire was the other Packets' mother. 'She's very good at organizing things.'

'Well, yes; they're coming over tomorrow afternoon for Porky's birthday party. I'll ask her about it and . . .'

'What did you say is happening tomorrow afternoon?'

'Porky's birthday party. Rose's guinea pig is a year old. She's invited her cousins, two rabbits and two other guinea pigs to tea. Oh, and a puppy.'

'Actually, I think I'll have to go to London tomorrow,' Father said hastily.

*   *   *   *

The children were allowed to read for a while in bed. Simon was reading a history book, and Rose was reading a book about guinea pigs and hamsters.

'What are plantains, Simon?' she called across the corridor. 'It says in my book they are good for guinea pigs.'

'They're weeds. They contain vitamin C, I should think.'

'What's that?'

'Like in spinach.'

'I think I'll give Porky some for his birthday tea.'

'But you've got masses of stuff already.'

'Yes, but he always likes a little something extra. He's a very hungry sort of guinea pig.'

'All guinea pigs are greedy.'

'He's *not* greedy—it's not true,' Rose shouted.

'Shall I tell you what I've been reading about Queen

Elizabeth?' Simon asked to change the subject. 'She was a terrible queen.'

There was a pause while Rose decided to forgive him for being rude about Porky. She never stayed cross for very long.

'Why was she a terrible queen?'

'She executed her cousin.'

'How dreadful. We wouldn't execute our cousin Felicity, would we?'

'No. And we wouldn't execute our cousin James.'

There was a short silence and then Rose said, 'Simon, what about our cousin Linda?'

Simon thought for a while and then sighed. 'Oh, well, maybe Elizabeth wasn't such a bad queen after all,' he said.

*　　*　　*　　*

Linda Packet was very like her mother, Claire. They both had short dark hair that curled tightly, they both had brown eyes and small mouths which, after they had finished speaking, they shut very tightly, so that you could almost hear a little click. They had a way of jerking their heads back too and sticking their chins out when they thought you might contradict them. Sometimes you didn't really think of contradicting them until they gave you this sign.

Only Linda and her mother came to the guinea pig's birthday party. Felicity had gone out to tea and James was too old for such things. Linda brought her rabbit; she carried it out into the garden and placed it in the pen with Porky, two guinea pigs from the cottage down the lane and another rabbit which lived nearby. Fortescue was in the middle of the run. He kept his head tucked in and did not move.

'He's only just come out of hibernation,' Simon explained. 'He is sort of thawing out.'

Rose carried out the birthday cake which she had made that morning. Its middle part was made of oatmeal, decorated with grated carrot. Round the edge she had written in chopped parsley, 'Happy Birthday Porky'. In the centre was a tiny carrot, shaped like a candle.

She put it down in the centre of the run. None of the animals took any notice. The rabbits were beginning to fight and the guinea pigs were nibbling grass.

'It's a bit mean, if you ask me, when you've gone to all that trouble,' Linda said disapprovingly. 'They might show some appreciation,' she added, tossing her head and sticking out her chin.

'That's all right,' Rose said. 'I don't mind.' She was disappointed all the same. She had imagined all the animals sitting round the cake just like a real party.

'What about *our* tea?' Linda asked.

Just then Mother brought out a tray of sandwiches and lemonade and they all turned their backs on the guinea pigs and rabbits and got on with their picnic.

Inside the house Mother told Aunt Claire about the French holiday.

'Of course they must go,' Aunt Claire said decisively. She always made up her mind about things very fast. 'It's an opportunity not to be missed.'

'Yes, but it's the journey. . . .'

'It's quite simple. After all, here we are in Dover, we should make the most of it. We just put them on the boat, then at the other end the train is waiting. They sleep all night and wake up at the station on the south coast of France where presumably your friend will meet them.'

'Yes. It *is* a very easy journey, but I'd feel happier if there was an adult travelling with them.'

'We can find somebody, I'm sure,' Aunt Claire said, tossing her head. 'The schools have French mademoiselles who must be travelling home at the end of the summer term. Leave it to me; I'll find somebody.'

Simon came indoors.

'How's the birthday party going?' his mother asked.

'Pretty boring,' Simon told her. 'One of the rabbits had a nose bleed and a guinea pig was sick. It's just like those awful parties for little girls that Rose used to have.'

'Oh dear, perhaps I'd better go and see if they're all right,' his mother said and went out into the garden.

'Aunt Claire,' Simon said. 'What do you think about the holiday in France?' He tried to sound casual and gazed at the stick insects as he spoke.

'It's all arranged. There are no problems,' Aunt Claire said and shut her small mouth firmly.

Simon forgot about being casual, gave a whoop of joy and dashed out into the garden.

Rose was bending over the run talking to Porky.

'We're going,' he shouted. 'We're almost certainly going.'

'Where?'

'To France, you idiot.'

'Oh, dear,' Rose said. 'But what about Porky? I can't possibly go to France and leave Porky behind.'

II

Departure

Once Aunt Claire had taken charge of the arrangements, everything was settled very quickly. She bought the tickets and made the bookings on the boat and the French train. It was the train that the children were particularly looking forward to, for they were to travel by sleeper all the way across France from Boulogne to St Raphael. She had arranged that the mademoiselle from the Girls' High School would travel with the children. All that Rose's mother had to do was to write to her friend Cynthia and say that they were coming.

'We're going to have to buy another case,' Mother said a week before they were due to go. 'You have one each, but I think you ought to have a spare case for warm things.'

'But it's going to be hot!'

'I know, Simon, but you can never be sure of the weather anywhere nowadays.'

So that afternoon Rose and her mother went into Dover by bus and bought a case. It was a big black one with N.P. in squiggly gold lettering just below the handle. The initials stood for No-Porter, the shop assistant explained, because it was so light. It was a very popular range, he added as he handed mother the change.

They were just crossing the road to catch the bus home

when they saw Aunt Claire's car. She waved to them and slowed down.

'Can't stop here,' she called out. 'But afraid to say that that Mademoiselle from the school has let us down. She's gone into hospital to have her appendix out, so she won't be travelling on our day.'

'Oh dear, poor little soul!' Mother exclaimed.

'You can't depend on anybody nowadays,' Aunt Claire said. 'But don't worry; I'll get somebody else.'

The car behind her was hooting.

'I'm going down to the docks to see if I can find anybody on the passenger lists who might be suitable,' Aunt Claire went on, ignoring the hooting. 'I'll let you know. All right, keep your hair on, I'm going!'

This last remark was addressed to the car behind. There was now quite a long queue of cars behind Aunt Claire. She set off and they all followed her in a long line.

*   *   *   *

Aunt Claire was as good as her word. The day before they were due to go she sent a message with James to say she had been down to the docks again and there met, by chance, a Mademoiselle Sourire who had agreed to escort the children. They would meet on the quay half an hour before the boat departed.

'Oh, what a relief,' Mother said to James.

James was their favourite cousin. Although he might have counted himself as grown up—for he was tall for his age and very sensible—he always treated them as if they were the same age as he was. One day, Rose supposed, watching him as he talked to their mother, he would really no longer be a child. He would desert to the adults, join the

17

other side. But for the moment he still belonged with them—Simon and her and Linda.

'Oh, what a relief, about that mademoiselle,' Mother said again after he had gone. 'I really couldn't have let you travel alone. Mademoiselle Sourire, what a pretty name!'

*   *   *   *

They were ready in good time on the day that they were to travel to France. Rose and Simon had each packed a case and Simon was in charge of the new case full of warm clothes. Rose had a blue grip full of paper and paints and books and a few games in case it rained. Simon was being allowed to borrow the family camera and binoculars and had them both strung around his neck. In addition to this, Simon had a hamper of food that Mother had packed and Rose had a string bag full of things she said she would need on the journey.

They stood in the living-room watching the road for Aunt Claire's car. She was taking them, Linda and James to the boat where she would leave them with Mademoiselle Sourire.

'The car, the car!' Simon shouted, snatching up the cases and making for the door.

'Don't forget anything,' Mother said. 'And write straight away when you arrive, won't you?'

'Yes, Mother,' Simon called back over his shoulder.

'I hope you've enough warm clothes. It's quite cold for July.'

'But it's hot *there*,' Simon called back.

'Well, mind you don't get sunstroke.'

She was still talking and worrying when they got into the car.

'And don't forget to say thank you when you leave,' was the last thing that they heard her say.

Rose sat in the back, squeezed between Simon and Linda, the string bag on her knee. She managed to twist herself round to wave good-bye. Her mother was standing by the gate, waving. Suddenly she looked blurred; it was awful

leaving Mummy, Rose realized, and would have done anything not to be going abroad. But then they went round the corner and she began to feel better.

Aunt Claire was a fast driver so it did not take them long to reach the docks. When they got out of the car, she said, 'Wait while I look around for Mademoiselle. Why, there she is!'

Rose could not see any Mademoiselle. The only person in sight apart from officials, was an old lady in black, holding a large black case, a black box, a black umbrella, and wearing a black hat with a veil. Aunt Claire seemed unperturbed. 'Mademoiselle,' she called, 'Mademoiselle Sourire!'

The old lady came across to them. She was introduced to each child in turn. Her hand was rough and bony and the skin felt loose, like a toad's.

It was quite difficult to see her face through the veil. She had a sharp, beaky nose, very bright eyes, bright red lips, thickly coated with lipstick, and wore a circle of rouge on each cheek. Behind the thick veil, she looked like a parrot in a cage.

'Come!' she said. 'We go now,' and, scarcely allowing them a moment to say good-bye to Aunt Claire, she set off. They followed her down the uneven gangplank and on to to the ship. Below them Rose could see coils of rope and engines and oily water.

Immediately they were on deck, Mademoiselle said, 'I always travel below. You stay here. I will find you in this place'—she pointed with her umbrella to a seat—'in two hours' time. Please not to lean over the edge.'

She walked away, taking her big black case with her. Rose noticed that it had a little gold N.P. sign on it, just like theirs.

She turned to Linda. 'Oh, I am glad she's gone,' she said. 'Isn't it awful? I mean she's not young. I thought she'd be a proper mademoiselle, didn't you?'

'I didn't think about it,' Linda said casually and shrugged her shoulders. 'It doesn't matter, does it? Look, we're off.'

The boat was slowly edging its way from the land. The four children watched as the white cliffs of Dover seemed to move away from them.

'How about something to eat?' James said, to cheer them up.

Linda and he began to unpack their picnic basket, which was a very grand one in red plastic. Simon undid the hamper and handed a sandwich to Rose. He was pleased with his sister. She had made less fuss than he had expected about leaving her guinea pig behind.

'You were jolly good about leaving Porky,' he said in the kind of voice that grown-ups use when they are pleased with you.

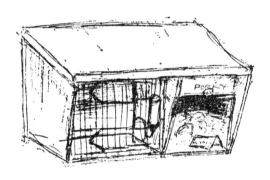

'I didn't,' Rose said.

He stared at her.

'What do you mean?' he asked, and his voice was hoarse.

'I've brought him,' Rose said, whispering so that the others would not hear.

'You can't,' Simon said. 'It's against the law.' Then he

added suddenly, 'Oh, Rose, you haven't packed him in the suitcase, have you? He'll suffocate.'

'No, he's in here,' Rose said, pointing to the string bag on her knee.

III

The Crossing

An hour later the four of them were sitting huddled together on the seat. It was much colder than they had expected, for the day was overcast and misty and the sea was grey. Wherever they stood or sat a cold wind blew straight at them.

An aeroplane flew overhead. They all looked up at it.

'I wish we were flying,' Linda remarked enviously. 'I bet it's warmer up there. And quicker. All I want is to get to nice warm France as quickly as possible.'

'What about hi-jackers?' James asked. 'Aeroplanes get hi-jacked, you know.'

'Well you could hi-jack a ship easily enough.'

'No, you couldn't.'

'Yes, you could. Think of it.' Simon lowered his voice and said, 'Two great swarthy men creeping up on deck. They look around. The passengers are taking no notice . . .' he indicated the men and women, the children playing, 'when suddenly the men snatch up two little girls . . .' he grabbed hold of Linda's hair and she shrieked. 'They lift them up and hold them over the side of the boat. "Listen everybody," they say, "If you don't hand the cap round and collect two thousand pounds in ransom money, we'll let go. They won't last long in the water you know, these little girls." '

Rose imagined it; she saw herself dangling by her plaits over the fathomless water; cold, terrifying, grey water, the string bag still hanging from her finger.

'Oh,' she said, 'and guinea pigs can't swim.'

James and Linda stared at her. Simon looked uncomfortable.

Then: 'Oh, Rose, you are an *ass*,' he said. 'You'd better tell them.'

So she told them about Porky.

'We're all likely to be put in prison,' Simon explained.

'Just like you to ruin everything,' Linda said furiously.

'Well, it's too late now,' James said kindly. 'But for goodness' sake don't let Mademoiselle know. When we get there we'll have to make a run in the shade. I shouldn't think it'll do any harm, it's a quiet place away from other animals, I expect. But you shouldn't have done it, Rose; you could start an epidemic. Disease, you know.'

'But Porky isn't diseased,' Rose said. 'He's the healthiest little guinea pig that ever lived. Look!'

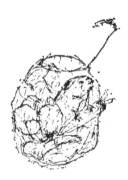

She rearranged the lettuce and carrots so that there was a little gap. Through this Porky peered out at them. For a moment he stopped chewing and stared at them with bright orange eyes. He blinked, wrinkled his nose and looked at them benignly. Then he went back to his chewing.

'I wonder what he thinks of it all?' Rose asked.

'Guinea pigs don't think,' Simon said scornfully. 'They just eat and sleep. You can tell by the expression on their faces that they're stupid.'

Rose stood up angrily, but before she could reply, Linda said : 'What about the customs? I expect you have to declare guinea pigs.'

Rose sat down again. She turned to James.

'Is it true?' she asked. She wasn't sure what declared meant but was fairly sure that it was nasty. It would be bad enough to be put in prison herself, but the thought of Porky being taken and declared was much worse.

James thought for a while and then he said, 'No, I don't think so. I mean it isn't as if you were going to sell him at a profit.'

'Certainly not,' Rose said indignantly. 'I wouldn't dream of such a thing.'

They all sat in silence for a while.

'Are we half-way?' Simon asked.

'Almost,' James said, looking at his watch.

In the distance Rose saw a shape looming out of the mist.

'France!' she shouted. 'Look, it's France!'

They all laughed.

'It's a lightship, silly,' Simon said.

She blushed and felt stupid. So later on when she did see what she was sure was land, she said nothing, and it was James who pointed out to them the first sight of France.

It was a long, straight-looking country, Rose observed. More like a model than a real place. You couldn't imagine

25

that there were real people there, real beaches and harbours. She would have liked to have lifted Porky up to have a look, but thought it was too risky.

'It's smaller than I thought,' Linda said, as they all stared at France.

'It's much bigger than England,' James said.

'Look, lovers,' Linda said.

By the rails, a tall, very dark-haired man had his arm around a girl, whose head rested on his shoulder. He was nibbling her ear.

'Soppy,' Simon said in disgust. 'Unhygienic.'

'French,' James said knowledgeably.

'I'd hit anyone who bit me in the ear,' Linda said.

'Sometimes Porky bites my ear when I pick him up,' Rose remarked. 'I suppose he thinks it's a carrot.'

The four of them sat staring at the French couple, who soon walked away and disappeared on to the upper deck.

The sun was beginning to break through now. It made the mist seem soft and floating and tinged with pink. It seemed to Rose that the boat was not moving in the water, but that France was drifting slowly towards them. Suddenly the gulls, which had been following at a distance, flew low over the boat. She wished she could paint it all; the gulls, the pink mist, the approaching green that was France.

'Expect they've thrown the rubbish overboard,' Simon said. 'That's what brings the gulls.'

People were beginning to move purposefully about. Parents were calling their children, assembling their baggage, moving towards the steps which led to the exit deck.

'Mademoiselle will be coming for us soon, I expect,' Linda said.

'I wish she was a *real* mademoiselle,' Rose said.

'But she *is*.'

'No, she's not.'

'Yes, she is. A mademoiselle is just an unmarried French lady.'

Rose gave up: she couldn't try to explain what it was about Mademoiselle that made her feel that she wasn't real. Perhaps it was just that she was so different from what she had expected. But when at last Mademoiselle Sourire did make her way, brisk, black, and heavily made-up behind her veil, Rose felt again a shiver of fear and distrust. She did not at all like the idea of spending the rest of the journey with her.

IV

Boulogne

It was a slow business getting off the boat; people were pushing and shoving and pressing against them as they followed Mademoiselle Sourire across the gangplank, on to the quay and down the slope which led to the station. James offered to carry Mademoiselle's case which Rose thought was very polite of him, as he was already carrying plenty of his own luggage. But Mademoiselle refused rather sharply and pulled the case in close to her side as if it contained something valuable which poor James was trying to steal.

There were a lot of people at the station. For the first time Rose realized that all around her French was being spoken. So they really had arrived : she felt suddenly excited and wondered what Porky was making of it all. She raised the string bag a little and stroked it, hoping to reassure him, but she did so very secretly in case anybody should see, especially the parrot-eyed Mademoiselle Sourire.

Immediately they had reached the platform and dumped down their luggage, Mademoiselle went to ask a porter about the train. Rose looked around; Boulogne station was surprisingly like an English station, she thought. And the weather wasn't much different either.

'I thought it would be hot in France,' she said.

'We're still in the north, silly,' Simon told her. He

was busy rearranging their cases to make a tidy pile.

'But it's still further south than we were at home,' Linda said, and she and Simon began an argument. That was the trouble with them, Rose thought, they were always arguing because they both thought that they were always right. She turned away from them and watched Mademoiselle talking to the porter. They seemed to be arguing too, both talking at once and waving their arms about. At last Mademoiselle came back to them.

'The train for St Raphael will come in two hours,' she said. 'I have in Boulogne an appointment to see my sister, so I will leave you here for a short time. You may walk by the water if you wish. If you are hungry you may eat some of your food, but remember to leave some for your supper on the train.'

'Yes, Mademoiselle,' they said, and she left them.

'She's ever so bossy,' Linda said.

'You can talk!' Simon told her rudely.

'Besides, she wasn't paid just to leave us like this,' Linda went on, ignoring him.

'*Paid*, she wasn't paid.'

'Yes, she was. I *saw* Mummy give her an envelope.'

'Oh, come on you two; stop arguing and let's go and look at the boats and eat our picnic.'

They walked across to the pier and sat down, their legs dangling over the water. All kinds of small craft were tied up below them; they were bobbing about on the water and their rigging was making a clattering sound.

'May I get Porky out?' Rose asked.

James looked around. There was nobody in sight.

'All right,' he said.

Rose pushed her hand into the bag. Then she gave a little gasp of horror; Porky was not there.

V

The Search

James took charge immediately.

'He can't have gone far, Rose,' he said cheerfully. 'Now just remember the last time you saw him.'

'It was just now. I looked at him and then—oh dear, I remember I put the string bag on the ground with the rest of the luggage. Only for a moment—but he must have wriggled out.'

'Then we'll start from where the luggage was, and we'll each go off in a different direction and just go on until we find him,' James said.

Even Linda didn't argue; they each went off quickly in the direction they were told.

Simon had to hunt towards the trains. Really, he thought as he walked along the platform staring at the ground, it was pretty hopeless. Porky might be anywhere. There was sea on one side and the river to fall into on the other. There was traffic in the town nearby and trains only a few yards away. Poor Porky. Of course, Simon thought, Porky was a nuisance and Rose was soppy about him, but all the same it was awful to think of him being drowned or run over. And there were so many feet, he thought as he pushed his way through the crowds.

A little passage led off the platform on his left. He

hesitated, not sure which way to go. It was a dirty little alleyway, full of dustbins and packing cases. At the far end was a big gate which presumably was opened sometimes to remove the rubbish. He stared down the passage and as he stared something white moved by a dustbin at the far end.

Telling himself that it was probably only a piece of paper, or perhaps a mouse, Simon ran towards it. As he reached the end of the passage, Porky emerged from behind the last dustbin and peered up at him. Simon lunged forward and

grabbed him. Never had he been so glad to see Porky.

It was then, as he straightened up, that he saw Mademoiselle. He stared at her in horror. She was only a few feet away from him, on the other side of the gate. If he moved she might turn round and see him crouching there, holding Porky. It was only a barred gate, which anyone could see through. Simon held his breath, afraid of making any sound, then a man came up and Mademoiselle Sourire immediately joined him and they went off together. They didn't speak; just walked away.

Simon let out his breath in a long sigh of relief. Then he dashed off to tell the others that Porky was safe. In no time at all they were once again sitting on the pier, and this time Rose held Porky on her knee.

'Jolly odd of Mademoiselle,' Linda said, 'to say she was going into Boulogne and all the time she was staying here at the station.'

'Perhaps she was waiting for her sister here and then going into Boulogne,' James suggested.

'But it was a *man* she met,' Simon pointed out.

'That could just have been a coincidence—I mean he may just have happened to see her by chance.'

'Well yes,' Simon said hesitantly, because he didn't really like to go on contradicting James, 'but she didn't seem surprised to see him. I mean if you meet someone by chance you usually look a bit surprised and say something, don't you?'

'Well, we've got Porky back and that's all that matters,' James said.

They forget about Mademoiselle and talked of other things. Porky sniffed the fresh air and looked about him with interest. The light breeze raised his brown and white fur very gently. Rose stroked him. She sighed contentedly.

It was all marvellous, to be in France and on holiday and to have Porky. It seemed almost too good to be true.

VI

The Sleeper

The train was bigger than any train that Rose had ever
seen. It was so high that they had to be helped up by an
attendant. The train and platform seemed suddenly to be
swarming with officials and porters and attendants, taking
tickets and telling them which sleeper to go to. Rose was
very glad that Porky was safely back in the string bag,
hidden away from all these people behind his lettuce leaves
and pieces of paper.

Mademoiselle had only just got back in time. She seemed
pleased with herself and spoke to them kindly. 'I'm so sorry
I kept you waiting,' she said again as they went into their
compartment. 'I had a little—er, business.'

She turned and talked quickly in French to the porter
who was carrying her case. He tried to put it on the rack
and nearly dropped it, it was so heavy. Simon helped him
to push it up. Rose watched him. She was often surprised
how helpful Simon could be outside the family. The case,
she noticed, had lost its little twisty N.P. sign. That is, if it
was the same case that Mademoiselle had taken with her.
Now that she looked more closely, it seemed a bit more old
and battered. She meant to point this out to the others, but
forgot about it.

They were in the girls' compartment; the top bunk was

already made up for the night with sheets, but the middle one had not been pulled out yet and the lowest one was still an ordinary bench. James, who had been on a sleeper before, explained that later an attendant would come and make these up into beds too. The boys were sleeping in the next compartment.

Suddenly the train lurched forward.

'We're off,' Linda said.

The train stopped. The children groaned.

Then the train started again and this time it did not stop. They sat back in their seats.

An attendant opened the door and rang a bell. 'Le dîner est servi,' he called.

'Now, children,' Mademoiselle said, 'I will be going to the dining-room car and you will be staying here for your picnic, that is so?'

They agreed and she left them. The children sighed with relief.

'I'm thirsty,' Linda said.

'I bet Porky is, too,' Rose said, taking him out of the string bag. She put him down carefully on the floor and he explored quietly, sniffing and wriggling his nose.

'You mustn't drink foreign water, it's poisonous,' Simon told them.

'How do the French manage then?' Linda asked.

'There'll be some in bottles,' James said. 'I say, let's look round the compartment, shall we, before we eat?'

They couldn't see that there was much to look at, but James soon showed them. He lifted up a wooden flap in the corner and under it was a little basin, with a tap.

'That's just washing water,' James said. He opened a cupboard above and showed them towels and a flask of drinking water. They all gasped at the neatness of it.

They unpacked the last of the picnic, which was beginning to look a bit old and squashed now. The orangeade was warm and the sandwiches were no longer flat. The cake was crumbly and the biscuits soft. But they were so hungry that it all tasted as good as new. As they ate, the trees and fields of France flew past the windows and the names of strange stations flashed by.

'You should say the names of things in French,' James told them.

'Like what?'

'Well, arbre when you see a tree and maison for a house, and so on.'

For a while they did this and then found that they kept seeing the same things. Fortunately it began to get dark so they had to stop anyway.

'I wish we didn't have Mademoiselle with us,' Rose said. 'Wouldn't it be lovely if we were by ourselves?'

'They wouldn't have let us come by ourselves.'

'We'd have been in a muddle at Boulogne without Mademoiselle to find the train and get the right sleepers and everything. I mean they gabbled like mad, those French station people.'

'I expect they think *we* gabble.'

'I hope she falls asleep in the dining car and spends the night there by mistake.'

'Don't worry,' James said. 'She won't come back for ages. The French take hours to have dinner.'

'Grown-ups are terribly slow about meals. They waste ages just sitting round the table even when it's finished. I shan't be like that when I'm grown up. I shall just gobble it up and go.'

'I bet you don't. You'll turn into a grown-up and be just as bad.'

'Shan't.'

'Bet you do.'

'Oh, shut up you two.'

They were interrupted by a rattling at the door and a man's voice shouted something in French.

Rose dived down under the bench and picked up Porky and pushed him back into the string bag.

'Vous permettez? On peut préparer les lits?' the attendant asked as he stood in the doorway.

They stared at James.

James stared at the attendant.

The attendant pointed to the bunks and made bed-making gestures with his arms.

'Oh yes, of course,' James said. 'I mean, Oui, monsieur.'

There wasn't much room in the compartment, so they all moved out into the corridor as the man set about changing the compartment into a bedroom. He undid straps and pulled the bench forward. He produced sheets and pillow-cases and very soon they could see three bunks, one above the other with tidy white sheets, all ready for them. The boys' compartment had been done already.

'I suppose we had better be on the top bunks,' Linda said, 'otherwise Mademoiselle will have to climb up over us.'

Rose shivered. 'I shouldn't like that at all,' she said.

'I don't expect she would either.'

'Let's go to bed now. Then we shan't need to talk to her.'

They said good-night to the boys, who seemed to have

38

their compartment to themselves. As they went along the corridor to the cloakroom they saw people coming up from the dining car. A very fat old Frenchman bore down on them. He had a half bottle of wine under one arm and in the other hand was holding a bottle of Perrier water. He looked very contented and a huge cigar was sticking out of his mouth.

'Golly, what a funny smell he had,' Rose said after he had passed.

'Brandy,' Linda said. 'Frenchmen drink lots of it—James told me.'

Rose gave Porky some more water, carefully taking it out of the carafe. Then they both washed, leaving the basin ready for Mademoiselle and climbed up into bed. They turned out all the lights except one tiny little one that glowed, so that Mademoiselle would be able to see her way around.

Rose was in the middle bunk. She stroked Porky, and put him carefully into the string bag, knotted the top very tightly so that he couldn't get out and settled him between herself and the wall of the compartment.

Soon Rose heard her cousin's quiet, regular breathing and felt sure Linda must be asleep. She whispered her name to make sure. Linda did not reply.

Rose lay still, enjoying the gentle rocking of the train, but too excited to sleep. It was lucky, she thought, that guinea pigs don't make much noise. If he were frightened or excited, of course, he would squeak, but in the quiet of the night he would be quite silent. Not like a cat that would set up a great purring which might puzzle Mademoiselle and make her suspicious.

She heard the door opening. She lay quite still, but by the soft glow of the nightlight she could make out Mademoiselle coming in the door. She brought with her a smell that Rose recognized : a smell of cigars and brandy like the man in the corridor. It seemed odd. Then she thought that perhaps in France women smoked cigars and everyone drank brandy. She would ask James tomorrow.

Mademoiselle put her bag down on the lowest bunk. She took off her hat with the veil. Rose could just make out the orange-pink colour of her hair. Mademoiselle went over to the basin and washed her hands. She seemed about to wash her face, for she ducked her head down and soaped her hands. Then she changed her mind, rinsed her hands and let the water go. She stooped down and Rose guessed that she must be undressing and getting into bed, but she was too far below her own bunk for her to be sure. Then there was a creaking sound and Mademoiselle settled into her bunk for the night.

For a long time Rose lay awake listening to the sounds of the train. They came to a station and stopped. She could hear a lot of shouting and through a crack at the side of the blind she could see brilliant lights. She realized that they were in Paris. She was surprised that the other two did not wake, for there was a great deal of noise and the train kept shunting in and out, and, as it did so, it rattled and shook. Mademoiselle was snoring loudly. She had a very loud, deep snore.

At last the train began to move steadily forwards and they left Paris behind. The long journey down to the south had begun. Rose thought how strange it was to be travelling right across a country and yet be in bed, and with Porky too. She felt as if they had the whole world to themselves. The train rocked them gently. Rose slept.

VII

Porky at Large

Porky slept well. When the light of early dawn began to show in the sky, he woke up suddenly. At once he felt very wide-awake. He sniffed; he could smell that it was morning and time to be stirring. He wriggled his nose. The carrot was all finished; there was a bit of lettuce left, but it was very flabby and he didn't fancy it. He peered out and the string rubbed against his nose. He gnawed at it absent-mindedly. It wasn't bad, he thought, not at all bad as string goes.

He ate some more. Really he was quite hungry, he thought, as he settled down to a good string breakfast. When he had finished he sat back blinking for a while. It was still dark, but the smell of morning was getting stronger. It made him feel restless. He had chewed quite a large hole in the string bag. He walked out of it.

He walked down the length of the nice soft thing he was on. Then suddenly something went wrong. The end gave way and he felt himself slipping. He managed to break the fall by hanging on to the blanket, and landed, fortunately, on something soft. Another bed just like the one above. But this one didn't have Rose on it. It had a different somebody altogether. Porky walked up and sniffed at its face. There was a terrific snort and the somebody sat up and yelled.

Porky fled. Down the length of the bed went Porky and hid in the corner.

Rose woke with a start. She put her hand in the string bag and realized that Porky had escaped. Without thinking

she put on the main light, saw that Porky was not on her bed and leant over, stretching her neck, and peered beneath her into the bunk below.

A strange sight met her eyes. Mademoiselle was sitting up in bed, glaring about, arms stretched out. They were rather hairy arms. She had just reached for a pair of spectacles, big, dark ones, like men wear, and had them in one hand, opened as if about to put them on. But the oddest thing was that her red hair seemed to have slipped and it was growing just down one side of her head.

'Oh!' Rose said in astonishment, staring at the bald head that had appeared underneath.

Mademoiselle reached up quickly and straightened the wig.

'It is nothing, Rose,' she said primly. 'I thought I felt an animal, that is all. A cat or something, but perhaps I was dreaming. Settle down; it is only five o'clock. Put off the light at once.'

Rose did as she was told. She lay very still. Poor Mademoiselle, she thought, she has to wear a wig because her own hair has fallen out. That's why she looks so odd. And she needs spectacles but thinks she looks nicer without. She felt sorry for Mademoiselle.

She soon forgot about Mademoiselle's wig and spectacles, however, in her anxiety over Porky. He must be somewhere down there. She hoped that he would have the sense to stay still until Mademoiselle went to sleep again and she could climb down and find him. She wished she had a torch. She wondered what Mademoiselle would do if she found out about Porky. She might tell the police. In that case she, Rose, would jolly well say, 'If you tell about my guinea pig, I'll tell about your wig.' Mademoiselle certainly minded a lot about her wig. She had looked jolly cross when she'd seen Rose's face peering in at her. Her make-up had been all smudged and her wig half off as she peered about. Rose shivered as she remembered.

At last she heard Mademoiselle start to snore again. Very gently she moved to the side of her own bunk and began to climb down. By the pale glow of the light she thought she could make out a little bump at the bottom of Mademoiselle's bed that could be Porky. Very gently she swung her leg over to the ladder and began to ease herself down.

To her horror just as she reached the ground, Porky ran up the bed, perhaps excited by the sight of Rose's legs coming down the ladder, and ran straight up to Mademoiselle's head. Before she could stop him, he had run across Mademoiselle's face. Mademoiselle jumped up and screamed again. Linda woke up this time and shouted,

'What is it? Burglars! Help!'

'Un rat, un rat,' Mademoiselle shouted with horror in her voice.

Porky had gone burrowing down the blankets.

'Allumez, allumez! Lights, children, lights,' yelled Mademoiselle Sourire.

At last Rose got her hands round Porky. She almost threw him up on her bunk and climbed up after him. Before the light went on she had pushed him back into the string bag and put a blanket on top of him.

'I'll come and help you look, Mademoiselle,' she offered politely.

'I'll get the attendant,' Mademoiselle said, and rang the bell.

Rose was horrified. She snatched up the string bag and climbed up into Linda's bed. 'You must keep him safely up here,' she said, 'and pretend to be asleep.'

The attendant came immediately and Mademoiselle and he had a long conversation in French. Then they took all the blankets off the bed and shook them. They peered under the bunks and even into the basin, but they found nothing. The attendant, who had been enjoying a nap in his chair in the corridor, looked tired and cross. She could see that he thought Mademoiselle had imagined it all.

'We've looked very carefully,' she called down. 'There's nothing at all up here.'

'Very well.'

At last the attendant left them. But Rose did not go to sleep again. Gradually the streaks of light in the sky grew brighter and the sun rose. Mademoiselle was snoring again, so Rose slipped out of her bunk and climbed up to Linda. It was a bit cramped, but they managed to sit up and mend the string bag with pieces of ribbon.

44

'The trouble is that he's hungry,' she said. 'That's why he ate the string.'

She reached up to a paper bag on the rack and found an apple. She watched, smiling, as Porky ate it hungrily.

'Poor little Porky,' she said. 'It must have been awful being yelled at like that. Rat indeed!'

'I'm not a bit sorry for him,' Linda said shortly. 'He should be back in his cage in Dover, where he belongs.'

Linda sounded quite astonishingly like her mother at times.

VIII

Rose in Danger

They got dressed and heard Mademoiselle moving about, creaking and breathing heavily. At last she called up, 'Time for the breakfast, girls. Are you ready?'

'Yes, Mademoiselle.'

They climbed down.

'Do you need to take your luggage?' Mademoiselle asked, pointing to the string bag.

'Yes, I think it's safer. I mean better,' Rose said.

Mademoiselle smiled. It was more a grimace really, but Rose knew that it was meant as a smile. She was trying to be friendly. 'It has something precious in, no doubt, child?'

'Well, my paints and things, you know,' Rose said.

'Ah, you paint pictures, do you? How amusing.'

She smiled again, a private smile this time. Rose did not see what was amusing, but laughed politely all the same.

James and Simon were waiting for them in the corridor and they all went along to the dining car together, swaying and bumping as they went. It was hot as they sat drinking big cups full of coffee that was so strong and bitter that it was impossible to drink it without pulling faces. Fortunately there were plenty of rolls and tiny little jars of jam to take the taste away. Through the windows they could see flowers growing in the fields, in rows like vegetables.

They made conversation politely, asking Mademoiselle the names of flowers. Then Linda said, to tease Rose, 'Could you tell me the French for guinea pig, Mademoiselle?'

Mademoiselle told her and added: 'They are good to eat.'

The children stared at her. 'Yes,' she went on, 'you just tap them on the nose and cook them with plenty of garlic.'

After that nobody felt like eating any more breakfast.

It was on their way back to their compartment, down the swaying corridor, that Rose nearly had the accident. She and Mademoiselle were the last. When the boys and Linda were out of sight, Mademoiselle stopped suddenly by one of the doors and pointed out to Rose how pretty the flowers were.

'This is an important area for flower-growing,' she said. 'For the perfume trade, you know.' Rose stopped and listened politely. 'Those grey-green plants are olives and those beyond are vines,' Mademoiselle went on.

Rose nodded and watched the fields go by. The colours of the lavender and olives and vines fascinated her. The greens were somehow different from the greens at home. She would like to try to paint them. She did not like standing so close to Mademoiselle, though, and kept her hand firmly on the string bag; she could just feel the warm fur inside it.

'It is very hot,' Mademoiselle said suddenly. 'I will open the window.'

She had been standing very close behind Rose and now leaned over her as if to lower the window. Rose saw Mademoiselle's hand move quickly down and suddenly the whole door flew open. There was a great rush of air and Rose felt herself thrown off balance. She could see the ground tearing past just beneath her and the wind dragged

47

at her. She clung frantically to the door frame, unable to cry out for the wind took her breath away.

To her amazement and despair, Mademoiselle, instead of trying to drag her back, seemed to be pushing her out of the train. Her arm was like a barrier which prevented Rose from getting back into the safety of the corridor. It was pushing her further, further out over the line. She could hear the noise of the great wheels clattering and grinding over the rails. Soon she would be flung out on to the line, she thought, almost sobbing with fear, for she could not cling on much longer.

She felt Mademoiselle trying to pull the string bag off her wrist and, glancing down, saw that the buttons of Mademoiselle's coat were enmeshed in the string bag. She and Mademoiselle were knotted together; if Rose fell out on to the line, they would both fall. So that was why Mademoiselle was trying to separate them by pulling the string bag off Rose's wrist. Rose gripped it desperately; she felt suddenly angry and very determined that whatever happened she was not going to abandon Porky to Mademoiselle, not after what Mademoiselle had said about eating guinea pigs.

Mademoiselle now gave up trying to drag the bag off Rose's wrist and instead began clawing at the string that was wrapped around her own buttons. As she tried to disentangle it, her arm relaxed and Rose made a great lunge and managed to duck under it, still clinging to the door frame, just as an attendant rushed down the corridor. He pushed them both roughly away from the door, shouting at them. Then very carefully he himself leaned out and got a grip on the handle and pulled the door closed.

It seemed suddenly very quiet. Rose did not know what to say. She removed the string bag from Mademoiselle's buttons and moved away from her.

The attendant was speaking sharply to Mademoiselle. She answered at length, waving her arms. He sounded more apologetic. She seemed to be blaming him for the bad catch on the door. He looked at it, he shrugged.

'Poor child, poor child,' Mademoiselle said, turning to Rose. 'It is so careless of the railways. They use these old

49

trains and do not check the doors. I have said I will report it. The attendant apologizes.'

Rose said, 'Oh, it's all right,' and went on down the corridor.

There was no need to go on about it, she thought, no need to fuss. She didn't know what to think. She couldn't really believe that Mademoiselle had wanted to push her out of the train, why should she? It must just have seemed like that. She shivered a little as she remembered the feeling of Mademoiselle pressing against her and the air rushing up. Mademoiselle's arm had felt as hard as stone, she thought. It was jolly lucky she'd had the string bag. Good old Porky; really he had saved her life.

She wouldn't tell the others, she decided. If Mademoiselle had wanted to push her out it could only be because she, Rose, had seen the wig, and she had already decided that she wasn't going to mention the wig to the others. Besides, it was too silly. Why should Mademoiselle be so cross about a wig that she would try to push anybody out of a train because of it? The others wouldn't believe her if she did tell them. They would laugh at her.

The children were quiet for the last part of the journey. It was a bit less exciting than they had expected. For one thing it was very hot and stuffy in the compartment. Then they were all feeling a bit squashed and tired. Their eyes felt dusty. They stared out at the flat countryside, at the fields of flowers, the neat rows of vines and olives, the little pink houses with thick roofs that seemed a bit heavy for them. It was all unreal, like something in a book. Mademoiselle was out of sight in the corridor. Rose slipped her hand into the string bag and laid it gently on Porky's warm fur, Porky was real anyway. That made her feel better.

'My eyes are full of bits,' Simon said and yawned.

'They don't look bitty,' Linda told him. 'Don't fuss.'

'I'm not fussing,' Simon said. 'Just stating a fact.'

He was beginning to feel jolly glad that Linda wasn't his sister. Rose was bad enough, all dreamy and potty about her guinea pig, but she wasn't bossy like Linda.

IX

Arrival

'Look,' James said, 'this must be St Raphael.'

Mademoiselle appeared in the doorway. 'Have you all your things, children?' she asked. 'It is time to dismount.'

Rose noticed that her face was newly made up, the lipstick very thick, the wig straight. She looked exactly as she had done when they had first set eyes on her at Dover. Last night she had seemed almost another person.

'What does your mother's friend Cynthia look like?' James asked Rose.

'Mummy said that she's about her age and tall and thin. Mummy said she always used to wear blue tweed suits and never went out without a hat.'

'That's not much help in this climate,' Simon pointed out.

'We descend now,' Mademoiselle said.

She was looking at Rose, who decided that she didn't want to be too near Mademoiselle, not after that near-accident with the door. She wasn't exactly frightened; she just didn't want anything unpleasant to happen to Porky. She squeezed in between James and Simon and the four of them moved out into the corridor with Mademoiselle bringing up the rear.

'Whew, it's hot,' Simon said. 'Don't *shove*, Rose. It isn't as if there's a rush. The train stops here for good.'

Rose had expected the station to be big and busy like Boulogne, but it seemed to be almost in the country. There were not many people about. They walked along towards the front of the train, where there were a few buildings, and Rose kept safely between Simon and James all the way.

Standing by the corner of the first building was a big brown man and a fair-haired girl wearing a short towel dress. She had huge round spectacles, long brown legs and sandals. As they walked past, she stepped forward.

'Could you be the Packets?' she asked.

They said that they were and then everyone began talking at once. Pierre, the big brown man, was introduced, and spoke to them in English which was very good, but obviously not quite right. Then he gabbled away to Mademoiselle and introduced his wife. They all shook hands and did a lot of nodding and what seemed to be thanking and not-at-alling. It struck her that the French were very polite to each other. Pierre explained that they were all to go to the restaurant at the station for a drink, but Mademoiselle refused. So they said good-bye and thanked her and followed Cynthia into the restaurant. Through the window Rose watched as Mademoiselle pointed to her case in the pile of luggage and Pierre picked it up and together they walked towards a parked taxi. She watched as the taxi drove round the corner and out of sight; she was very glad to see the last of Mademoiselle Sourire.

They sat around the table in the restaurant drinking fresh lemon juice. Now that she could see her more closely, Rose realized that Cynthia was older than she had thought at first. But she still seemed much younger than her mother. She tried to imagine her mother in a very short towel dress with brown legs and long hair down her back. She couldn't.

'Oh, it will be lovely to have you,' Cynthia said. 'I'm sorry that we don't have any children of our own for you to play with.'

'Oh, don't worry about that,' Simon assured her. 'We didn't come here to play.'

Cynthia smiled. 'Of course not,' she said. 'You must forgive me—I'd forgotten that you are all quite old and grown-up.'

Pierre came back. 'Eh bien,' he said, sitting down next to Cynthia. 'So these are our English friends. I'm sorry your Mademoiselle would not stay, but she seemed eager to be gone. I should have liked to have given her a little entertainment for the day to show how much we appreciate her help. But the moment I suggested a swim and picnic she went away very fast indeed.'

They all laughed. Rose liked them both, this nice new young aunt and the funny old Uncle who looked as if he might be her father. Already she knew that they weren't going to treat the four of them like schoolchildren.

'Well, in that case,' Cynthia said, getting up, 'let's go

straight up home and get you settled into your caravans. I've put lunch ready; I expect you're all starving.'

As they piled all their luggage into the boot of the car, Cynthia said, 'You won't want to hold that string bag on your knee, will you, Rose? I'd shove it in the boot.'

Rose looked at James in dismay, then back at Cynthia.

'If it's very precious, take it with you of course,' Cynthia said.

Rose did.

X

There at last

'You'll have to tell Cynthia about Porky,' James whispered to Rose in the car. 'She's very nice, I'm sure she'll understand.'

'Er, yes, but she *is* a grown-up, all the same.'

But she knew that she must tell. It was too dangerous to risk Porky catching sunstroke or being shoved into the boot and having a case plonked on top of him by mistake. The first time she was alone with Cynthia, she decided, she would confess all about Porky.

Once they were out of the town, the road began to climb very steeply between hills, twisting and turning as it went. At first there was just grass and rocks to be seen on each side, but gradually there were more and more trees and finally the road wound among pine-forests. There was a lovely gummy kind of smell.

They drove for about an hour and then Pierre turned down a bumpy lane.

'This was once a railway line,' he explained. 'And here we are,' he added, turning sharply down a drive on the left.

At first they did not see the house, for there were a great many trees and long grass and it was all very overgrown. When her eyes took in the cottage at last, Rose gasped; it was quite beautiful. It was like something in a picture book,

with its pale pink walls, and its roof of darker pink tiles, made out of what looked like pipes cut in two.

'Your caravans are in the field through that gap in the hedge,' Cynthia said as they got out of the car. 'Pierre will help you unload, while I go and collect the lunch from the house—perhaps one of the girls will help me?'

'I'll come,' Rose said quickly.

Cynthia led the way down the path and into the house. Rose followed in silence. She knew that this was her chance to tell Cynthia about Porky, but she didn't know how to begin.

'Aunt Cynthia,' she made herself say.

'Don't call me Aunt, whatever you do,' Cynthia interrupted as she opened the front door. 'It makes me feel so old. Just Pierre and Cynthia, we'd like you to call us. The kitchen's this way.'

'All right. Well, Cynthia,' Rose started again. She looked around the kitchen, at Cynthia taking things out of the refrigerator, at the squirly patterns on the tiled floor. There was wrought-iron at the windows and all the wood was an orangy-coloured pine.

Suddenly Cynthia turned round and looked at her seriously.

'Just tell me quickly,' she said. 'It's much the best. Don't think about it. Just talk.'

So Rose did just that. She told her all about not wanting to come to France because of Porky and how she had written a note to her mother and left it in the cage and packed Porky up in the string bag. She didn't look up because she didn't want to see Cynthia's face turn angry. She went on about the night and how Porky had got out and Mademoiselle had called the attendant and said that there were rats in the train. Then she stopped. Cynthia was doubled up with laughter.

'Oh, my goodness,' she said. 'I can't wait to tell Pierre.'

'But you see,' Rose said, now really anxious because Cynthia had misunderstood. 'It's against the law and if the police found out, they'd put him in quarantine for six months, which is a very long time for a guinea pig because their whole life is so short . . .'

Cynthia stopped laughing and took her hand. 'Don't worry,' she said. 'It won't happen. Of course you shouldn't have brought him, but it's done now, so we must just make him as comfortable as possible. May I have a peep?'

Rose drew aside the apple peelings and paper and Porky peered out at them. He blinked and chewed and looked very friendly. Rose felt very proud of him.

'He's beautiful,' Cynthia said. 'Pierre will make a run for him after lunch. Meanwhile you'd better keep an eye on him, knowing how good he is at eating string.'

She began to laugh again, as she collected the picnic up into a big basket and led the way out of the house.

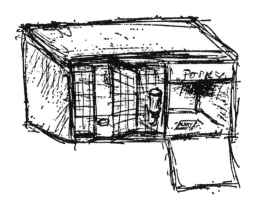

XI

The Caravans

Rose followed Cynthia through the gap in the tall hedge, and found herself in a field, which fell away in terraces down to a low wall at the bottom.

'Those are lavender fields down there, the blue hazy ones,' Cynthia said. 'They use it in the scent factories. Pierre's family is in the scent trade. But you haven't noticed the caravans—look up there.'

Rose turned to look where she had pointed. At the top of the field, up on her right, she saw two caravans under the trees. They were not modern ones, but not quite gypsy caravans. They were painted red and white and had checked gingham curtains at the windows. Between them and further back under the trees was a little outdoor kitchen. It leant up against an old stone wall and was open at the sides, the roof being supported on poles at each end.

'You'll find everything you need in there,' Cynthia said. 'I don't expect you'll want to do very complicated cooking. There's a tap just round at the side.'

On the old stone wall there were wooden pegs from which hung big iron pans. There were tins of supplies and a cooking stove, which Pierre was busy explaining to the boys.

'While you unpack I'll put the lunch out on the table under the aleppo pine,' Cynthia told them.

'We won't want those hot clothes,' Simon called across to Rose. 'I've shoved the new case under my bunk.'

She thanked him and went to unpack.

Linda was in the caravan already.

'I'm having this bed,' she told Rose. 'It's nearer the door if there's a fire.'

Rose didn't mind. From the window by her bed she could gaze out over the terraces, and lavender fields, and across to the distant hills. Anyway, she couldn't see any reason why there should be a fire in the caravan.

It was hot. They unpacked as quickly as they could, and put the empty cases on top of the cupboard.

'That was quick,' Cynthia said. 'I can see you're not time-wasters.'

'Rose is,' Linda said. 'She's a dreamer.'

On a little round table under a pine tree Cynthia had spread out plates and glasses, lettuces, huge tomatoes, a bottle of wine, cheese, iced lemon juice, a long loaf of bread.

'Help yourselves,' Cynthia said. 'Before the butter melts.'

They were ravenously hungry. Gradually the full plates were emptied until there was nothing left except peach stones and orange peel and a generous scattering of crisp golden breadcrumbs by each place. Pierre emptied the wine bottle into Cynthia's glass. He sighed contentedly.

'And who will be cook when you start on your own?' he asked.

They decided that the girls would do it one day and the boys the next. The ones who did the cooking would do the shopping in the village in the morning and prepare the meal, but not wash up.

'That's jolly mean,' Simon said, 'because the girls will

make all sorts of messy things, you bet, and we'll have to wash up. We'll just make bread and cheese, and that's easy to wash up.'

Pierre laughed. 'Well, we'll take you to the village this evening,' he said, 'and show you the shops. By the way, there's an apricot tree down there on the lower terraces, and several plum trees. There is the remains of a vegetable garden behind that wall where you can pick anything you like, though I'm afraid it's all a bit overgrown, like everything else here.'

Cynthia must have found time to tell Pierre about Porky because immediately lunch was over, he began making a run. Rose chose the place, at the back of the caravan and under the trees where it was shady all day. Pierre was very good at making things. In about half an hour he had made a run out of stiff wire, with a wooden box at one end where Porky could shelter if there should be a shower. They found some straw for him in case it was cold at night, and old plates for his food. Lastly they made a strong frame to fit on the top, which lifted off when she wanted to get Porky out.

'We're off to our siesta now,' Cynthia said. 'But if you like we'll go to the village later and show you round. Then from tomorrow onwards, you're on your own.'

It had an exciting sound, on their own. On their own. Just the four of them—and Porky.

XII

The Village

The way to the village was along the disused railway track, all overgrown with wild thyme and sage, so that the smell of the herbs rose all around them as they walked.

'We'll need milk and bread and butter for breakfast,' Rose said.

'And cereals, and bacon and eggs . . .'

'Oh, no, Simon,' James objected. 'In France they just have bread and butter and—oh, can we get cherry jam, Cynthia?'

Cynthia laughed. 'You can get what you like,' she said.

After that they all began saying all their favourite things to eat. They were still making lists when they reached the village.

The village was perched on the side of the hill, like an eagle's nest. The houses seemed to have been built into the rock of the hillside and every street was narrow and steep. After they had done the shopping they climbed up to the very top where there was a square with a fountain and a restaurant with little tables outside. There they sat and drank lemon juice and watched the people passing by.

It was getting dark as they walked back. When they reached the cross-roads where the old railway track met the road from the village, Pierre pointed to a path on the left.

64

'That is the way down to the lake,' he said. 'It is good swimming there—very safe.'

'James and I both have our life-saving badges,' Linda put in, tossing her head. 'So you needn't worry about us.'

Rose thought she sounded rude, but Cynthia only laughed and said, 'Good. I'd heard from your mother that you all swim like fish.'

'Let's go to the lake tomorrow,' James said, and they all agreed.

They were quiet as they walked back along the railway line, for they were beginning to feel very tired. The smell of herbs was strong and the air heavy. In the distance an owl screeched. Rose jumped and was glad that Porky had a cover on his run.

They all helped to get the supper and sat eating it by moonlight under the aleppo pine. They watched the stars coming out, one by one.

'You're almost asleep already,' Cynthia said, as they cleared away. 'We'll be off now, and let you get to bed. Remember that tomorrow you'll be fending for yourselves.'

They said good night and tried to thank Cynthia and Pierre, but it was difficult to find words which were good enough for such a marvellous holiday.

After the grown-ups had gone, Rose went to settle Porky down for the night. He was crouched on the straw blinking up at the moon. She picked him up and stroked him gently. 'Tomorrow we're fending for ourselves,' she told him.

'I wonder if he realizes that he's in France?' Linda asked, coming up behind Rose.

'Of course he does. He saw when we crossed the sea.'

'What did Mademoiselle say that the French called guinea pigs?'

'I've forgotten,' Rose said. She didn't want to remember

c   65

anything which Mademoiselle had said about guinea pigs. In fact she was quite happy to forget about Mademoiselle Sourire altogether.

'Do you know,' Linda said later, as she and Rose were washing under the tap, 'it's almost as light as day.'

It was true. The moon hung, almost full, in the sky just above the caravans, and the stars were brilliant. Everything, the caravans, the terrace walls, the little house down in the valley, all seemed very clear and distinct. But it was different from daylight. It was clear, but as if painted only in shades of grey, or black and white, like a photograph. Then there was an extra something too, a kind of eeriness. In dreams, Rose thought, didn't things look like this? Perhaps there aren't colours in dreams. She couldn't remember. Next time I dream, she thought as she climbed up the steps to the caravan, I must notice. But she fell asleep the minute she put her head on the pillow and did not dream at all that night. Or if she did, she didn't remember in the morning.

XIII

The Lake

One of the advantages of living in a hot place is that you do not have to waste a lot of time getting dressed. The children were up and about very quickly the next morning. It was still early when they set off for the lake, James and Simon carrying the picnic, Rose the swimming things and Linda her new snorkel and mask which had been a birthday present that summer.

It was all right walking in the shade along the old railway line, but once they reached the road it was very hot, and they had to walk slowly and with their heads down.

'Whew!' Simon said. 'I wish we were at the lake. I could just do with a swim.'

James laughed. 'Look,' he said. Right in front of them was a sign which read: 'Au lac' and pointed down a little path. They forgot about being hot and dashed down it.

The path made its way down a steep slope between pine trees. They slipped and skidded all the way, hanging on to the branches of trees. Suddenly James stopped. Simon, who was close behind him, fell over. They all laughed except Simon, but even he forgot to be cross when he stood up and saw what James had seen. Just below him lay the lake; it was pure blue and glittering in the sunshine. There was nobody else to be seen; just the white sail of a single boat in the middle of the lake.

They didn't speak, just ran the rest of the way, and within five minutes were in the water.

'I like it better than the sea,' Rose said, as the four of them swam lazily in the sun. 'Water's better without salt.'

'And beaches get very crowded,' Simon said.

'Oh, I don't agree at all,' Linda said. 'I like having plenty of people about and I don't mind salt either.'

'You always have to disagree with everybody, don't you, Linda?' Simon said and splashed water all over her.

'Oh, you beast! Look what you've made me do. I've dropped the mask. I had it in my hand.'

'More fool you! You should have had it on. Anyway I'll get it.'

Simon dived, but came up without it. They all dived and churned up the water, which just there was quite weedy and muddy.

'It's all your fault,' Linda said furiously to Simon. 'You're always fooling about. Silly idiot.'

'Oh, don't fuss. I'll get it back for you,' Simon said, trying to sound confident, though they all knew it was pretty hopeless trying to see under the water now.

'If only we had a mask,' Rose said, 'we could see better.'

'If we had the mask we shouldn't be hunting,' Linda snapped.

'I only meant . . .'

'You're as silly as Simon.'

'No, she's not,' Simon said. Then they all laughed, except Linda who was too cross to see a joke.

'We might buy another,' Simon said.

'No, we've only just enough money for food,' James said. 'Come on, try once more.'

Rose came up first, the other three were all under the water with their legs waving about. It was then that she noticed the boy.

He was swimming towards them from the boat and he was wearing a mask. The others had all surfaced by the time he reached them. He spoke to them very fast in French and they all looked at James. Then James and he spoke in

69

a mixture of French and English and made all kinds of signs. The boy disappeared under the water. He came up with Linda's mask. Linda tried to thank him in French and looked confused and not at all like their usual bossy Linda. But then the boy, whose name was Alain, spoke a bit in English and they spoke a bit in French, and made signs, and in no time at all they were playing together and had no difficulty in understanding each other. They swam and snorkelled and explored the shore. Alain explained that he lived in Paris but his father had had to come here to work for a while, so his mother and he had come too and were staying in the village. At lunch time he left them as his mother was expecting him at home, but he promised to come again next day.

The four of them settled down by the side of the lake to eat their picnic. Other people had come by now but there was still plenty of room.

'I'm absolutely starving,' Simon said, eating a boiled egg and a great hunk of bread.

'How did you get on at the shops this morning?' Linda asked.

'James was jolly good. Honest, he sounded just like Pierre—well, almost.'

'Rose and I are going to shop on the way home. We're going to buy peppers and tomatoes and . . .'

'Do you know the names of them?'

'No, we'll just point.'

'That's not much good for your French,' Simon told her. 'Just going around pointing.'

They lay in the sun, arguing and eating peaches. Rose looked across the lake. You couldn't call it blue, not really. If you painted it, you would need quite a lot of white and some dark grey, but in the end it would have to look like blue altogether. She wished she had her paints with her. But in a way she was glad just to sit, holding her knees and gazing across the lake and now and then sucking a juicy peach.

The day slipped by, swimming, eating, getting hot in the sun and cooling off in the water. At half past four they set off for home. It was cooler now but under their clothes their skin felt warm and glowing.

That evening Cynthia and Pierre came over to see them.

'How are you managing?' Cynthia asked. 'Any problems?'

They all spoke at once, assuring her that there were none.

'In that case,' she said, 'I think it will be all right if we go, don't you, Pierre?'

'Go?'

'We were asked to go and see some friends for the week-end at Nice. Well, for four days really, starting the day after tomorrow. Actually they asked us a while ago, but I thought I'd like to be sure you could manage on your own before we left you.'

'We like managing by ourselves, really we do. Please don't worry about us.'

'Well now, I've written down the name and address of where we shall be, and of course we'll see you again before we leave. Oh, by the way, here are some apricots off our tree.' She nodded towards a newspaper parcel which she had left on the table. 'But do help yourselves in future—the trees are laden. Well, enjoy yourselves.'

They went away and the children talked excitedly.

'I think it's super the way they trust us to look after ourselves,' Linda said.

'The only thing is that it's going to be horrible going back to England and being treated like children again.'

'Don't think about it—let's have an apricot.'

They helped themselves.

'Oh, aren't they lovely? Much better than the tinned ones. Look, they're wrapped up in an old English newspaper. I didn't know you could get English newspapers in France.'

'Of course you can, silly. I expect Cynthia and Pierre get one every day.'

'This one is the 28th—the day we left.'

'Does it have about us in it?'

They all laughed.

'Just boring grown-up stuff,' Simon said, reading out the headline. 'Art treasures stolen from London Gallery. International gang suspected.'

'What are art treasures?'

'Pictures, I suppose.'

'Why can't they say so? Chuck it away, Simon. We don't want to think about England and school.'

'School, ugh!' Simon exclaimed, screwing up the newspaper.

XIV

The Storm

The days followed much the same pattern. They didn't have definite meal times, but just ate when they were hungry, swam when they were hot, drank when they were thirsty and came home when they were tired.

But the day after Cynthia and Pierre had left them, there was a change. It was hot when they went off to the lake, but by midday the sky had darkened.

'Incredible though it seems,' Simon said as they sat eating their picnic, 'I think it could rain.'

'Yes,' James agreed. 'Look at the lake.'

The smooth surface of the lake was ruffled by little waves and ripples. They had never seen it like that before.

'It looks like half-set jelly,' Linda said.

'Trust you to think of food,' Simon told her.

'Alain said he thought there might be a storm,' James remarked.

'Oh dear, what about Porky?' Rose asked.

'Never mind Porky,' Simon said. 'What about us?'

'Porky will be all right,' James said. 'He'll stay down under the covered end of the run.'

They packed up quickly and set off for home. Just as they walked into the field the first big drops of rain began to fall.

That afternoon they played cards and scrabble, in the boys' caravan, and the rain beat down outside. It was almost impossible to see through the windows; it was as if a moving curtain of grey was between them and the field outside.

Suddenly there was a flash of lightning. Rose cried out. Simon told her not to be a baby.

'But it's Porky,' she said.

'It isn't,' Simon insisted. 'You were scared.'

'I'm going to get him,' she said.

'I'll go,' James said.

He put a towel over his head and opened the door and dashed out through the rain.

'If James catches pneumonia it'll be your fault,' Simon said.

Rose didn't reply. She knew that when Simon was in a disagreeable mood he only got worse if you contradicted him.

In a few minutes James was back with the guinea pig under the towel.

'Oh, thank you very much,' Rose said. 'Oh, look at poor Porky—he's shaking. Never mind, Porky, it's all right.'

After that Porky stayed on her knee while they played. At last the rain grew less. They opened the door and looked out.

'Everything's soaking,' James said. 'We'll have to have supper in here.'

'Shall we get some warm things out of the case we shoved under the bed?' Simon asked. 'You know the big black one with the socks and trousers?'

They got up off the bed, lifted up the cover and pulled out the case. Simon lifted it up on to the table and opened it.

'What do you want out, Rose?' he asked. 'I'm getting my socks and—golly!'

They all turned to look. Simon had lifted up the lid and was staring, completely stupefied, into the case. The other three peered in too. They couldn't believe their eyes.

XV

A Mystery

The case contained no socks or jumpers or clothes of any sort. It contained rolls of thick paper, which looked rather like cloth.

Simon unrolled one and smoothed it out.

'It's a painting,' he said.

Linda leaned over him and glanced at the other rolls.

'They're all paintings,' she said. 'They're not yours, are they, Rose?'

Rose, who didn't get up because she had Porky on her knee, shook her head.

'Perhaps it isn't your case,' Linda suggested.

'I think it must be,' Rose said. 'Mummy and I bought it in Dover.'

'Of course it's our case,' Simon agreed. 'Besides, I remember pushing it under here.'

'But it hasn't your things in it, it can't be your case,' Linda insisted. 'Perhaps somebody stole yours and put this one in its place.'

'But why should anybody want *our* case? Just a lot of tatty old socks and jumpers. Nobody here would want English winter woollies.'

'*My* jumper wasn't tatty, it was quite new.'

James held up his hand.

'Now don't go off the point. The main thing is to think it out clearly. There must be an explanation. If it got exchanged by mistake at the station, then it must be Mademoiselle's. Her case was just like that one. She went off in a hurry, you remember, and either she—or more likely Pierre —picked her case from the pile of luggage outside the restaurant. Right?'

'Right,' they agreed.

'So, by accident her case and ours got swopped over. She's got our clothes and we've got her paintings.'

'Right.'

There was silence for a while.

'But then, she knows our address,' Simon objected. 'The moment she opened that case and found all our things in it, why didn't she ring Cynthia and explain and swop the cases back?'

'And why was she travelling with nothing but rolls of paintings? I mean I could understand it if she'd had a case of clothes as well, but this was all she had except that little box thing, her umbrella, and . . .'

'I've thought of something,' Simon shouted again.

They all jumped.

'I know it sounds mad, but when the porter came with us to the girls' compartment, he really had a bit of a struggle getting Mademoiselle's case on the rack. It was quite heavy, I'm sure it was.'

James looked at him doubtfully. 'Are you sure, Simon?' he asked. 'Because I certainly noticed that Mademoiselle carried it very easily off the boat. It looked so big that I offered to carry it for her and she snatched it up and wouldn't let me.'

'I'm quite sure,' Simon said crossly.

'All right. Then she must have put something in it when she went off at Boulogne on business. She may have gone shopping.'

'She might have bought an iron or a hammer or something, and packed it to save having a separate parcel,' Simon agreed.

Rose looked up from stroking Porky.

'But,' she said slowly, 'she didn't.'

'Didn't what?'

'Put something heavy in her case at Boulogne.'

'Then what did she do?'

'She changed cases.'

They stared at her in disbelief.

'But she went away with a big black case and came back with the same one,' Simon said.

Rose shook her head.

'The case she came back with didn't have a little gold

thing on saying N.P. I noticed that hers did—like ours—at Dover. I thought perhaps it had fallen off. But when I looked a bit harder, I saw that the case was older; it seemed a bit more battered, somehow.'

'I didn't notice any difference,' Linda said. 'I bet you've only just thought of it.'

'Rose *does* notice things. She's dreamy, but she sort of notices little things,' Simon said. He spoke a bit awkwardly. He didn't mind being rude to Rose himself, but objected to Linda doing it.

'Well then,' James said. 'To start again. Assuming that Rose is right, Mademoiselle left Dover with a light case— light in weight, I mean, not colour. Then at Boulogne she meant to swop it with another case almost exactly the same but without the N.P. sign. But by mistake she picked up your case. After all, we did put them all down together on the platform.'

'Oh, and I remember rearranging them a bit while she was asking that chap about the trains,' Simon said suddenly.

'So she took our case at Boulogne by mistake, leaving this one—' he pointed to the case on the table—'with us. She then went off and swopped our case—thinking it was hers with the paintings in—with the heavy one which you later saw the porter heaving on to the rack.'

'I wish we knew what she did at Boulogne,' Simon said.

'We do. She swopped cases,' Linda said. She felt a bit left out of things. The others seemed to have been doing all the remembering.

'But why? People don't usually bring a case over from England and then swop it for a different one the minute they arrive in France.'

'Perhaps she was fed up with carrying those paintings about. Maybe she meant to give them to her sister.'

'I bet her sister got a fright when she found my socks instead of Mademoiselle's beautiful paintings!' Simon exclaimed and shouted with laughter.

'She'd have got more of a fright if you'd worn them,' Linda told him rudely. 'Anyway, I'm starving. What's for supper tonight?'

'Ask no questions and you'll be told no lies,' Simon said, because he did not know.

James stood up and stretched. 'Yes, time to cook,' he said. 'We'll just have to leave the paintings here until Pierre and Cynthia come back. Meanwhile we'd better just shove them back under the bed.'

They nodded. Now that the mystery was solved, it no longer seemed very important.

The boys went out to the kitchen. Linda began to set out a game of clock patience for herself on the table.

Idly, Rose went over to the case, took out the painting from the top and unrolled it. She found herself looking down into water, ripply water with whites and greys and movement. Almost it felt wet, she thought, touching it gently. There was a boat in the water and in it a girl was sitting, her hand trailing in the water, her face turned towards the light of the sun. The light was in everything. It didn't just shine from the sky as in most good paintings. It was reflected off the boat, off the girl's face, but above all off the water, the lovely, living, moving water. In one corner the picture was signed *Manet*, which Rose supposed to be Mademoiselle's Christian name. As she gazed down, she forgot the caravan, the night, the other children. She had never seen anything like this painting by Mademoiselle.

XVI

Rose's Picture Gallery

After breakfast the next morning, Rose asked James if she might take the case of pictures over to the other caravan to look at them properly.

'Of course,' he said. 'You take them. You're the only one of us who can paint, so you might as well enjoy them.'

'Actually from what I saw of the wishy-washy things,' Simon said, 'I think yours are every bit as good as hers, Rose.'

Rose blushed and thanked him. Then she took the case in one hand and Porky in the other and went over to the caravan.

While the boys went to the village to shop and Linda played patience on the table under the pine trees, Rose settled down to look at the pictures. Her hands were trembling as she opened the case, she was so excited. Gently she unrolled the top one, the one which Mademoiselle had signed *Manet*, and laid it on the bed. Then she took another picture out of the case and unrolled it. She gasped. In a field of corn an old man was standing, but it was the corn that was astonishing. It was golden, unbelievably bright and soft and real, moving in the wind. Really you could almost feel it moving. For a moment the caravan seemed to be filled with its golden light. Gently she laid it on the bed.

The next picture was a street scene. You could see that it was raining: there were umbrellas and people, all wet, all hurrying. She knew how they felt: she had felt like that herself, hurrying through the rain from school, not the driving sort of rain that makes you feel alive, but nasty, drizzly sort of rain, that makes the road look slippery. The street looked so slippery that she could almost feel the oiliness of it.

Picture after picture she unrolled and laid on the bed. She couldn't bear to shut them up in the case, she thought, taking a box of drawing pins from the cupboard. She would pin them all round the walls of the caravan. Surely Mademoiselle wouldn't mind that? The edges were damaged anyway: it looked as if Mademoiselle had once had them framed. Certainly they were good enough to frame, Rose thought. She wondered why Mademoiselle had taken them out of their frames. Maybe they were easier to carry back to France that way.

At the foot of her bed she pinned the first one she had seen—the one with the girl and the boat. She stood staring at it; if only she could one day paint like that herself, she thought. But it didn't really matter; just so long as somebody could paint like that, that was the main thing; that pictures like that should get themselves painted.

She walked slowly round the caravan looking at each one in turn. She heard Linda coming.

'You've been ages,' Linda said. 'What are you doing? Oh, you've pinned them up. That's nice. It was a bit bare before. I thought of picking some flowers, but they'd die in the heat. Let's have a look.'

They walked together round the caravan, looking at each painting in turn, as if they were in an art gallery.

'Let me see which I like best,' Linda said. 'I think that

84

one—the one that says "Renoir" in the corner. What about you?'

Rose thought hard. 'Honestly I don't know,' she said slowly. 'If I could only have one I suppose it would have to be that one, the one that says "Manet" in the corner.'

'Yes, I like that too. I suppose they must be places, Renoir and Manet and things?'

'I suppose so. At first I thought it might be her Christian name, but there are so many different ones.'

'It doesn't say Sourire on any of them,' Linda said, looking carefully.

'Who would have thought Mademoiselle could paint like this?' Rose said. She felt a great sense of awe and respect for the little French woman with the black hat and red wig.

'Oh, I don't know,' Linda said, turning her back on the paintings and going out of the door. 'They're all right, but a bit blurry. I think yours are every bit as good.'

Rose followed her, shaking her head. It was jolly nice of Linda to say that, she thought, but really it wasn't true. These pictures of Mademoiselle's were really quite different from anything she herself had ever painted.

XVII

Uninvited Guests

'It's a bit late to take a picnic lunch,' James said when the boys got back from shopping. 'Let's have it here and then go to the lake this evening. It's going to be hot again.'

'Super—let's have a midnight swim.'

'All right—but let's not wait till midnight. It's dark by eight o'clock. We can swim by moonlight.'

They all thought that this was a marvellous idea. In fact it was one of those days when everybody agrees with everybody else and nobody argues. After lunch the boys went exploring, Linda read a book and Rose sat at the round table trying to paint the view across the valley. They set out for the lake after tea.

'Just think, we've been here a whole week,' Simon said as they walked along the railway line. 'It doesn't seem possible.'

'Oh, I don't know,' Linda said. 'I feel as if it's years and years since we left Dover.'

'Back to normal,' James said.

'What do you mean?'

'You two arguing. It's been quite odd up till now—you haven't had a single quarrel all day.'

Simon looked a bit sheepish, but Linda just said, 'Well, he always starts it.'

As they scrambled down the path to the lake they met Alain and his mother coming up.

'Oh, please can Alain stay?' Simon asked, and they all joined in.

Alain's mother laughed and said of course he could stay, but she must go home and prepare his father's evening meal. So the five of them went tracking in the woods, ate their picnic and, as the moon rose, dived into the lake. The water was cold, and they had to swim vigorously to keep warm. But it was very beautiful under the moon, absolutely still and mysterious.

'It must look like this every night when we're asleep in the caravans,' Rose said.

'And nobody to see it,' Linda exclaimed. 'What a waste.'

When they got out, the woods seemed eerie and frightening. The moonlight drained the colour from the trees and turned their branches into menacing arms. Rose was glad when James said they must pack up and go home.

'Will your parents think you're very late?' James asked Alain. 'It's past ten o'clock.'

'No, we go quite late to bed when we're on holiday,' Alain reassured him.

'We'll walk home by the village and see you home.'

To their surprise there were still quite a few people about in the village, and some were still sitting at the tables outside the restaurant, too, enjoying the warm night air.

'This is where we are staying,' Alain said, stopping outside a wrought iron gate. 'Will you enter?'

They said they had better get back, but arranged to meet at the lake the next day. Then they walked quietly home, not talking because they were suddenly tired.

They were just turning into the drive of Cynthia's house,

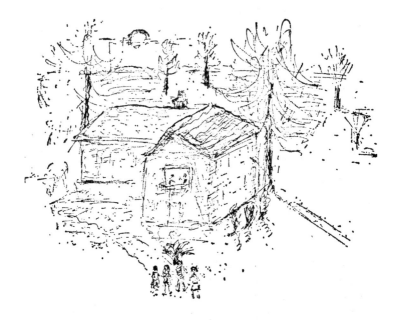

when James stopped suddenly. 'Quiet everyone,' he hissed, and pulled them back into the bushes.

They looked where he was pointing. A small light was moving about inside Cynthia's house.

XVIII

Two Strange Men

For a while they were silent, waiting for James to tell them what to do.

'I think we should creep nearer and try to see what's going on,' he said at last.

Quietly, stealthily, they crept through the overgrown garden. They paused at the side of the house, where they could see through the hall and into the sitting-room. From there they could see two men. They were evidently hunting for something, for they were moving about the room, not making any mess, but searching very thoroughly. They looked under chairs, on bookcases, examining all the bigger pieces of furniture.

'It's queer,' James said. 'They're not ordinary burglars. They're not just stealing things.'

'Yes, it's as if they're looking for one special thing,' Simon agreed in a whisper.

The men sat down and began to talk.

'If we could get round to the big window, the one with the view across the valley at the back, we might be able to hear what they're saying,' James whispered.

The others nodded. In single file they crept round to the back of the house and crouched in the long grass below the window.

From here they could see much better. One of the men was very small and bald. The other was big and swarthy. They could hear the murmuring of their voices but could make out nothing of what the men were saying.

For a long time they crouched there listening. Every now and then the others looked hopefully at James, but he always shook his head. They withdrew into the bushes to discuss what they should do.

'It's hopeless,' James said. 'My French just isn't up to it. They seem to be arguing. Often the big one asks the little one questions and gets angry when he doesn't get the right answers—at least that's what it sounds like.'

'I wish we had Alain here,' Simon said.

'You're a genius,' James exclaimed. 'Why didn't I think of Alain before?'

'And he said he went to bed late,' Simon pointed out excitedly, 'so his parents won't mind.'

'Don't you think we ought to get the police?' Rose asked timidly.

'No,' James said. 'After all, we don't know for sure that the men have no right in the house. We don't want to cause an upset and spoil Cynthia's holiday all for nothing. But Alain will be able to tell us. I'm off now. You three get near enough to keep an eye on what they do and I'll be back soon with Alain.'

He vanished into the bushes and the other three returned to their position in the grass under the window. They could see the light moving from room to room as the men continued their search. Every now and then they returned to the living-room and talked and then, as if they had had another idea, went off again. There seemed to be no pattern in their coming and going.

Rose shivered; they had never been out so late and it was

surprisingly cold. Suddenly the light vanished and this time did not reappear. Rose crouched very still; it was frightening not knowing where the men had gone.

'Where do you think they are?' she whispered to Linda.

'I think they may have gone out of the front door,' Linda whispered back.

They both looked at Simon. He moved nearer to them. Even the long grass seemed to make a dreadful crackling sound, so still was the night. If only it had been daytime, Rose thought, there would have been the constant shrieking of crickets and cicadas to cover up their own sounds.

'I think we'd better stay here for a while,' Simon said. 'I'm pretty sure they must be going out up the front drive now, but you never know. They may have got suspicious and be hunting the grounds.'

'They might meet James and Alain,' Linda said casually.

Rose felt a sickening lurch in her stomach. She imagined the boys walking down the road and meeting those two men, burglars or whatever they were. Or worse still, if Alain hadn't been allowed to come, James would be alone. She got up suddenly. 'We must go and help James,' she said.

'Get down, you idiot,' Simon said, giving her a shove.

'But he'd just be one against those two,' Rose said trying to get up.

'Of course we must help him, but quietly. We'll crawl

through the long grass to the bushes at the side of the house, and then creep round to the front.'

Rose was about to reply when, hearing a sound, she looked up and saw, only a yard or so from her, two pairs of boots appear through the grass.

She tried to scream, but only gave a little gasp.

XIX

Eavesdropping

'Sh,' James said. 'It's only Alain and me.'

He settled down beside them in the grass.

'How did you find us?'

'The row you three were making; it was enough to wake the whole village!'

'I know,' Simon said, 'the girls were fussing and squawking about rescuing you. I just couldn't keep them quiet.'

'Oh, shut up, Simon. Tell us what's happened, James.'

'Right, Linda. It's all right—we can speak up a bit now. They've gone. Well, Alain and I came quietly back, keeping in the trees in case we should meet them. Just as we got within sight of the house, we saw the light go out of the sitting-room and move into the hall. Then it went out and very quietly the front door opened. They stood for a while, then flashed the torch round a bit in the bushes—fortunately not too thoroughly—and walked up the drive and down the road. They must have had a car hidden not very far off. We stayed hidden until we heard an engine start up.'

'So Alain was too late to hear anything?'

'No, they were talking as they walked up the drive. Tell them what you heard, Alain.'

Alain hesitated for a moment. They knew he was trying to find the right English words. They knew how he felt—just like they did in shops. They waited patiently.

'They were 'aving a quarrel,' Alain began. Rose shivered; Alain's broken English, spoken in a whisper in the dark, was very eerie. 'Zen one said to the other, "Ow could you be so stupid?", and ze one wizout ze hair, he said, "It was your idea to make me wear zat ridiculous disguise and wizzout ze spectacles I can nothing see." Then the big man said, "Well, it is your fault, so you must be the one to find it. Now, if not 'ere, where is it?" '

'Didn't they say what "it" was?'

'Never. I listened very hard and never did I hear what "it" was. I tried to make out if they might mention a ring or jewels or any such thing, but they never did.'

'I think it must have been something pretty big they were looking for,' James said thoughtfully. 'I mean they weren't pulling out small drawers and making a mess emptying cupboards the way ordinary burglars do.'

'Did they say anything else, Alain?' Simon asked.

'When zey were almost at ze top of ze drive, standing very close to us, ze bald man said, "I just don't understand where zey can all have gone. Zere is no trace of zem in ze house." '

'*All* of them?' Rose queried.

'Exactement,' Alain said, breaking into French with excitement. 'They do not know your friends Pierre and the lady with the difficult name . . .'

'Cynthia,' Linda supplied.

'Cynsia,' Alain repeated. 'Neither of these men know your friends or they would surely know they have no children. Twice they spoke of *all* of them, as if there was a big family.'

For a while the children sat in silence.

Then James said, 'We're very grateful to you for coming, Alain, I'd never have made out what they were saying.'

Alain laughed and shrugged. 'I neither would understand English in whispers and fast like that,' he said.

'Let's go back to the caravan and decide what to do.'

Alain looked at his watch. 'Nearly midnight,' he said. 'Thank you but I go back now. I think you have to tell police tomorrow.'

'I suppose so,' James said. 'But we didn't want to make a fuss.'

'Oh, ze English never like fuss, zat is what we are told.'

'Well, when we thought they might possibly be friends of Cynthia's and Pierre's, we thought we shouldn't interfere, but now that we know they can't know them—well, it does look as if they might be thieves.'

'We could always ring them up . . .'

'Oh no,' Simon said, 'they'll think we're frightened and come back. It would spoil their holiday.'

'I agree. We're not frightened, are we?' Linda said.

'Of course not,' Rose said quickly, though really she was.

'Alain,' James said, 'we'd never be able to explain to the police. Do you think . . .?'

'Of course, tomorrow we'll go together.'

He hesitated, and then went on, 'I should tell you perhaps that my father is Le Commissaire de Police—'ow do you call it in English?—Superintendent of Police—in Paris. It is for investigation of a case that he had to come down here.'

The children listened in amazement.

'We'd no idea,' James said.

'I did not tell you because my father prefers it so,' Alain explained. 'But now I tell you because sometimes he visits the policeman in the village and you might meet with him there tomorrow. Of course, this matter of the burglars will be for the village policeman to deal with.'

95

'Of course. So we'll meet you at the police-station, so that you can help us explain?'

'Oui. We meet in the square, yes?'

'Right. And afterwards we'll go to the lake together as usual?'

'Splendide. At what hour?'

'Shall we come about nine o'clock? Then we'll go on together to the lake, unless the police want us to come back here or anything.'

'Splendide,' Alain said again. 'Bonsoir tout le monde.'

'Bonsoir, Alain,' they replied.

As they walked over to the caravans the moon lit up the pine tree so that its branches were like great black arms above their heads. Even the kitchen, hunched under the trees, seemed sinister.

'You girls all right in your caravan tonight?' James said casually.

Linda laughed. 'Why ever not?' she asked. 'We're not scared.'

But Rose noticed that she locked the door and closed the little bolt, which they did not usually bother to do.

'I'm not going to go out and wash,' she said.

'Neither am I,' Rose agreed. 'After all, we've swum so late today, we must be jolly clean.'

'Just what I thought,' Linda said. 'And I expect eating those apples cleaned our teeth.'

They both jumped into bed and pulled the sheets up around their ears. For a while when she shut her eyes Rose imagined she could see the light as it moved from room to room. Then she imagined the faces of the men and shivered. There was something about the bald one that was puzzling, but she couldn't think what it was. At last her eyes saw only blackness and she slept.

XX

Kidnapped!

It was a lovely morning. The air was fresh, the sun brilliant.

'Don't let's waste too much time with the police,' Linda said.

She adored the lake and didn't want to risk having to spend hours in some police station while James and Alain answered questions.

'It won't take long,' James told her.

'Well, to save time I'll go shopping while you boys are with the police,' Linda said.

'Shall I stay here and get the picnic ready?' Rose volunteered.

'That would be super,' James told her. 'You don't mind being alone here, after last night I mean?'

Rose laughed. 'Course not,' she said. 'It's daylight!'

She walked with them to the railway line and watched them go. Then she went back to the kitchen to prepare the picnic. She washed the lettuce and tomatoes, she wrapped up cheese and ham and peeled the eggs which were already hard boiled. Very gently she took five peaches from the box, and packed them carefully into the basket. Then she took the outside leaves of the lettuce over to Porky.

'Here you are,' she said, stooping down to take the cover off the run. Porky looked up gratefully. She stood and watched him as he nibbled. It seemed suddenly quiet without the others. She looked behind her. She hoped that they wouldn't be long.

She picked Porky up for company. He climbed up and lay against her shoulder. She walked over to the caravan, stroking him and talking quietly. 'I'll show you our pictures, Porky,' she said as she climbed up the steps.

She held him up in front of each picture, telling him what she liked about each one. Gradually she forgot about being alone, forgot everything except the pictures. Gently she put Porky down in a cardboard box full of straw which was always at the corner of the caravan, and went back to the pictures. She stood for a long time staring at the one with the umbrellas. It was the sheen of water on everything that was so amazing, so entrancing, she thought, and turned to look at the other picture, the one with the boat. As she turned she heard a sound and glanced towards the door, expecting Linda.

Two men stood in the doorway. She stared at them, unable to move. They stared back at her. She felt her mouth go dry and her stomach felt funny. Then her mind seemed to go very clear. She knew them, she recognized them; they were the men who had been in the house last night, but they did not know her. They did not know that she had seen them. So long as she just pretended that she thought they were friends, they had no reason to harm her.

'How do you do,' she said politely.

'Er, bonjour,' the big man said. The other one stared at the ground.

'If you wish to see Pierre and Cynthia they are away from home,' she went on. Then she wondered if perhaps that was foolish. No need for her to let them know she was alone. 'The boys are about somewhere,' she said, 'in the other caravan, perhaps.'

A look passed between the two men. Neither spoke.

'Au revoir, Mademoiselle,' the big man said politely and began backing down the steps.

Rose moved forward, ready to see them out, and then bolt the door. As she did so, the bald man saw the picture behind her. He gave a loud exclamation and said something to the big man, who also stared and stood still in the doorway. They looked around the caravan, from picture to picture as if stunned. Rose smiled and nodded to show that she was pleased that they liked the pictures but would like them to go away now.

Then a strange thing happened. Above the door of the caravan was a glass panel. It was made of a kind of orange-pink glass which, Rose imagined, was designed to stop too much sun getting into the caravans, which were very hot. It made a queer kind of light on anything just below it. Just at that moment the bald man moved slightly, so that the pinkish-orange light fell direct on to the top of his head, making it seem as if he had red hair. At the same time he looked up and caught Rose's eye, which he had been avoiding hitherto; he gave a nervous smile.

It was the red light and the false smile that did it.

'Mademoiselle Sourire!' Rose exclaimed.

Everything happened at once. The bald man rushed forward and put his hand over her mouth. Rose yelled and tried to push it away, the big man slammed the door closed and bolted it. He took some twine from his pocket and before she realized what he was doing had seized both her hands and tied them behind her back very tightly, and had put a scarf over her mouth. He said something to the bald man who rushed at the pictures and began pulling them down.

'Doucement, doucement,' the big man said and Rose realized that he was telling Mademoiselle—or whoever he or she was—to be careful with the pictures. She was glad of this, partly for the pictures' sake and partly because she felt sure that anybody who didn't want to hurt pictures would be unlikely to do much harm to her. All the same she wished that the others would come back. If she could get her arms loose surely the five of them—she hoped to goodness that Alain did come back with them—would be a match for the two men?

The big man snatched up Linda's case from the top of the cupboard and was stuffing the paintings into it. Then he pointed at Rose and began giving orders to the bald man and she realized that they were preparing to take her with them. Horror filled her. Also bewilderment. Why, she wondered, did she matter to them? She couldn't hurt them. But of course, it was because she had recognized Mademoiselle. They knew that she could go straight to the police and explain that Mademoiselle was a criminal in disguise.

The big man indicated the door. The bald man said, 'Walk.' For a moment she wondered if she could leave a trail like people did in books. If she asked permission to leave Porky in the run, she might manage to scribble a note as she did so, but she couldn't risk drawing attention to Porky, whom in their haste they had not noticed. She knew too well how Mademoiselle thought of guinea pigs. So she said nothing. They pushed her down the steps, across the field and into a waiting blue car.

She delayed them as much as she could, pretending to fall, walking as slowly as possible, anything to waste even a few minutes to give James and the others time to get back. But there was no sign of them as the fat man opened the car door and the bald man pushed her in and slammed it behind her.

They set off immediately, the big man driving. Once they were driving at speed, the bald man turned round and took the scarf off Rose's mouth.

At first she stayed where she had fallen on the back seat, but once she realized that they didn't want her to attract attention, she sat up quickly. She couldn't wave because her hands were tied, but perhaps if she pulled terrible faces, somebody would notice. But there was nobody on the deserted road.

It occurred to her that the other children would not even realize that she had been taken away. She imagined them coming back. They'd call out her name a few times, look in the caravan, but then they'd say, 'She's gone for a walk, silly old thing. She's gone dreaming off. We'll just have to wait until she gets back. Bother.' And they'd wait and wait. She felt tears prickle her eyes. She might never see any of them again.

The pictures! They would surely think it a bit odd that the pictures had been taken down. If they noticed. She had to admit that the others didn't share her great joy in the pictures. She herself would have noticed straight away if the paintings had gone from the caravan. It would be as if a great light had been turned out. But they might not. Or if they did they might just shrug and say, 'Rose has got sick of those pictures. She's put them away and is going to paint some better ones herself.'

But of course they'd see Porky. They would know that she wouldn't just go and leave Porky like that, cramped up in the little box; if she had gone for a walk, they'd say, she'd have taken him or put him in the run. Yes, the presence of Porky would tell them that she had not left the caravan of her own free will, Rose thought, and began to feel more cheerful.

XXI

Meet the Police

Linda had finished her shopping. There was no sign of the
boys in the square, so she went and knocked on the door of
the police station.

Alain, James and Simon were sitting at a table with two
Frenchmen to whom she was introduced. One, who was
called Monsieur Lebrun, had a cheery red face and spoke

almost no English. He was the village policeman. The other, Alain's father, was tall and thin. He spoke very good English indeed, better even than Pierre.

'Please sit down, mademoiselle,' he said, drawing up a chair for Linda, who sat down rather grandly. 'I was just telling your brother and cousin that their description of these two men interests me. They sound like members of a gang of international thieves we are trying to track down. But how about something for you children to drink first?'

He went to the door and summoned the waiter from the café opposite, who soon brought a tray with long glasses and straws, which he set down in front of them. There was a clinking sound of ice cubes against glass.

'Tell me about yourselves,' the Superintendent asked as they began to drink. 'How did you travel—alone?'

'No,' James said. 'We had a French person.'

'Ah,' the Superintendent looked very interested. 'A man?'

'No, a lady,' James said. He looked at his watch; he was beginning to think it was a bit mean sitting here drinking iced lemon juice while poor old Rose did all the work back at the caravan. It was all right when they were doing something that mattered like reporting the men last night, but now they were just chatting it didn't seem right at all.

'Describe this lady to me.'

They all joined in a description of Mademoiselle Sourire.

'And had you known her long?'

'We didn't know her at all,' they said, and James explained how his mother had met Mademoiselle Sourire at the quay only the day before they travelled. At this the Superintendent turned and talked quickly to the policeman who nodded.

'C'est possible,' he said.

'What's possible?' Linda asked Alain.

'That mademoiselle was a man in disguise.'

They all stared in amazement.

'Did she carry anything?' the Superintendent asked. 'Describe her luggage please.'

They looked at James.

'Well,' he began. 'It sounds a bit silly, but we think she took one of our cases by mistake at Boulogne and swopped it for another.'

'Why do you think that?'

James hesitated. After all, they didn't mind about losing a few clothes. He didn't want the Superintendent to think that they were fussing about it when there were much more important things for him to worry about.

'Well, you see, when we looked in our case it didn't have our warm clothes in it any more—it should have had Simon's socks and . . .'

'What did it have?' the Superintendent interrupted.

'Well, nothing really. Just a few paintings.'

The Superintendent stared. He did not jump up. He did not shout. But James had a funny feeling that that was what he would have done if he had not been a Superintendent of Police.

'Vite,' he said, 'En auto!'

He led them out to the cars parked in the square. The boys went ahead in the Superintendent's car and Linda followed with the policeman. None of them had any idea why it was so urgent.

'Can you see the house and the caravans from the road?' the Superintendent asked the boys.

'I don't know,' James said. 'We always walk along the railway track at the back.'

'Well, look out now and tell me when you see it.'

'There, up there,' James said almost immediately. Across

the lavender fields on the left, they could just see the house and beyond the trees and bushes, the two caravans in the field.

The Superintendent nodded. 'Yes,' he said, 'it would be quite possible for them to have located the house from the road. Then this morning they could go back and look again from here and see the caravans.'

Simon shivered; it was awful to think that they might have been spied on this morning by the very men they had themselves spied on last night.

The Superintendent drove very fast now; he stopped the car just short of the turning to the caravans. The policeman parked behind him. James thought he saw the tail of a blue car driving away, but he wasn't sure, so he didn't mention it.

XXII

Detective Work

Although she was no longer gagged, Rose sat in silence in the back of the car. The two men occasionally said something to each other in French but mostly they too were silent. The big man concentrated on driving fast and the bald man sat clutching the case of pictures and staring at the road in front of him.

It was the way that they had pulled down the pictures and rushed off with them that puzzled Rose. Of course, she quite understood that anyone who had painted such marvellous pictures would want them back, but why had it been so urgent? It seemed queer that Mademoiselle—she still thought of him as Mademoiselle—had cared quite so much about the paintings.

It occurred to her that perhaps Mademoiselle was mad. After all she had tried to push her off the train just for knowing about the wig. Suddenly it struck her that if Mademoiselle was prepared to kill her just for that, she had even more reason to do so now. She was so frightened that she spoke without thinking.

'Where are we going?' she asked.

'To look at a very splendid view,' the bald man answered and laughed.

He then translated her question and his answer for the

big man, who did not laugh, but just grunted. It seemed to Rose that the big man thought the bald man a fool. Once or twice he had called him stupid; she had caught the word 'bête' in their conversation.

Suddenly the two of them talked rapidly in French. Then the bald man said to her, 'You told lies when you said your brothers and sisters were in the caravan. They were not. Where are they?'

'I don't know,' Rose said.

'We watched them go,' the bald man said. As he spoke he glanced at the shelf in front of him, where a pair of binoculars were lying. He did it unconsciously, but she realized at once that the men must have watched them this morning through binoculars. Last night they had searched the house, this morning they had realized about the caravans and decided to search them too. That was it. They had stood in the lavender fields and watched the children through binoculars. They had seen them leave and thought they had all gone. She had walked out into the lane with the others, she remembered now, and then returned, by which time the men were no longer watching. No wonder they were so surprised when they found her there. Not for the first time she wished with all her heart that she had gone with the others to the village that morning.

*   *   *   *

The four children and two policemen stood in the field. It looked deserted. In the kitchen the picnic was all put ready.

'Perhaps she has gone for a walk,' Linda said. 'She does sometimes. She likes to dream along by herself. Oh, look, Porky's gone.'

'Well, let's look in the caravans.'

The boys', of course, was empty. They walked over to the girls' caravan. Linda said, 'Ah, the door's open. She must be in.'

It was one of the rules always to leave the doors closed when they went out, in case a wind got up and pulled the door back on its hinges.

They climbed up the steps and into the caravan. It seemed crowded with six people in it. They were so squashed together that nobody noticed the bare walls.

But Linda found Porky.

She stooped down and picked him up. She looked over his head at the others. For the first time, she was worried. 'Rose wouldn't do that,' she said.

'What?' the others asked.

'Leave Porky all alone in a stuffy old caravan.'

'Perhaps that's why she left the door open.'

Linda shook her head. 'No, she'd have put him in the run and shut the door. I'm positive.'

The Superintendent was looking puzzled.

'Tell me about this Porky,' he said.

They all looked at the ground. Nobody spoke. It occurred to Linda that perhaps the special investigation that the Superintendent had come for was to do with smuggled guinea pigs. She shut her mouth firmly, determined not to give Rose away.

'Quickly,' the Superintendent said. 'We have no time to waste.'

So, reluctantly, James had to tell the truth about Porky and how Rose had brought him over from England in the string bag.

'She didn't want to leave him behind, you see,' he ended.

'She's very fond of him,' Linda explained. 'He's a very nice little animal.'

'And it isn't as if she was spreading illnesses to other guinea pigs,' Simon said.

The ghost of a smile flickered across the Superintendent's face. Then he looked serious again. 'So you are sure she would not go away of her own free will and leave behind the—what did you say—piglet from Guyana?—in the box?'

'Positive,' Linda said again. 'And the word's guinea pig.'

James blushed. Nobody but his sister, he thought, would dare to correct a police Superintendent.

'Thank you, mademoiselle,' the Superintendent said, bowing slightly to Linda. 'Now we must follow them.'

'Follow them?'

'Follow whoever has taken your sister.'

'But who would take Rose?'

'Whoever you saw last night. I will explain in the car. But first is there anything different in here? Any sign of a struggle?'

They all looked about the caravan, except Linda who stroked Porky. Somehow now that this awful disaster had befallen Rose, it seemed very important to look after Porky for her.

'Nothing's different is it, Linda?' James asked.

'No, I don't think so,' Linda said, looking around. 'Oh, she's taken all the paintings down.'

'You mean the paintings were *here*, Mademoiselle?'

'Yes, you see Rose pinned them all up . . .'

'Describe them.'

'Well, Rose could tell you better. There was one with a girl in a boat and one with umbrellas. They were places. They had the names on like Manet and Renoir and. . . .'

The Superintendent's mouth opened and shut. At last he managed to say, 'And you had these, these, these *masterpieces* pinned up in this *caravan*?'

'Yes,' Linda said. 'With drawing pins. Rose likes pictures.'

XXIII

The Gorge

It was very uncomfortable sitting with her hands tied behind her back, but Rose was determined to sit up as tall as possible so that she would be able to pull frantic faces at anyone she saw. But she knew that they would only catch a glimpse of her as the car flashed past, they wouldn't be able to save her. Anyway, the road was deserted.

She concentrated on watching the route the car was taking. It was a familiar road now, the same that they had driven along when Cynthia and Pierre had taken them for an outing to a famous gorge, the day before they went away. She recognized a narrow bridge, a castle perched on a cliff, a viaduct across a valley.

Cynthia had thought that it would be a treat for them to see the gorge and the boys had loved every minute of it. Rose had not liked to say so, but she had hated it. The road had climbed so high that it was eventually built into the side of the mountains; on one side the rock face rose straight up and on the other it simply dropped away into a sheer abyss, into nothingness. Even the memory of it made Rose feel quite ill. She loved mountains, she didn't mind when they towered above her, but she hated looking down into ravines. There was something about the way her eyes had to travel down, down, down that made her feel sick and dizzy.

Pierre had parked the car at a viewing place, a bluff of land sticking right out above the gorge. They had all got out and walked along the grass to the very edge. The boys had thought it was marvellous; they had stood there for ages looking down. Pierre had told them how deep it was in metres and they had stood there on the very edge translating the metres into feet and arguing. Rose could not stop thinking that one step would take them over the edge and falling, falling into the abyss. It was terrifying; it could easily happen. A false step, or a little push.

From the viewing point they had been able to see the road winding ahead, for it had been blasted out of the rock of the mountainside. Sometimes it went right through the mountain, disappearing into a tunnel and emerging at the other side. It did not seem possible that men could have made it; they must have been clinging to the rock face like spiders as they worked. Simon said it was a great feat of engineering and Pierre had said several men had been killed making the road.

Feeling sick, Rose had gone back to the car. 'Don't you like it?' Cynthia had asked her kindly. She had lied of course and said it was beautiful and she loved it, but Cynthia had said never mind, she got gorge-sick herself sometimes too.

How long ago that outing with dear kind Cynthia and Pierre seemed, Rose thought. Her eyes filled with tears as she remembered them. She told herself that crying wouldn't help and made herself sit up very straight and look as brave as she could, so that the men would not see that she was afraid.

The bald man had taken out a map and the two of them were talking hard as if making plans. They were certainly on the road to the gorge, Rose thought with sinking heart, as she recognized the countryside that flew past the car windows. And the road was getting steeper and steeper. She had thought the bald man was joking when he talked about showing her a view, but perhaps that was what he had meant. Perhaps they were going to take her up to the dreadful viewing point. And then what?

XXIV

Explanations

Simon climbed into the passenger seat of the Superintendent's big black car. The others were behind in the policeman's car, which was to follow more slowly. Nobody noticed that Linda was still holding Porky when she climbed in. Or if they did, they didn't mention it.

'I wanted you in with me,' the Superintendent said to Simon after he had checked that his safety belt was properly fastened, 'because you are Rose's brother. If we should catch a glimpse of their car, you are the one most likely to recognize her, her clothes and so on.'

Simon tried hard to think what Rose had been wearing today. He could not remember. He had a vague idea that she usually had on something pink with stripes. Sometimes she wore her hair loose, sometimes in plaits. He couldn't remember how it had been this morning. He had an awful feeling that Linda would probably know better than he did what Rose was looking like today.

'Fortunately there's only one road out of here,' the Superintendent went on. 'Get the map out will you—it's in front of you on the shelf.'

Simon reached forward and spread the map out over his knees. Although he was driving so fast, the Superintendent managed to point to places on the map with his right hand as he talked.

'If my guess is right,' he said, 'they'll make for this route into Switzerland. They won't want to go by the main routes like the coast road, as they'll know all the frontier posts are watched by the police. They will try to get over the mountains. It could be Italy, but we think Switzerland's more likely. Either way, I have a feeling they will go up by the gorge.'

Simon was trying hard to understand.

'You mean they'll try to take the paintings from the caravan abroad?'

'We think it's possible. You see the pictures were stolen from an exhibition of Impressionist paintings in London. They were great pictures borrowed from galleries and collectors all over the world. After the robbery the police were tipped off that it had been organized by an international gang and that a Frenchman would be bringing them over to France. We guessed it would be by boat, so all the ports were watched and every Frenchman checked.'

'Oh, I'm beginning to understand now why you think Mademoiselle Sourire might be a man in disguise.'

'Precisely. How pleased he must have been when he was asked to bring you over. What better disguise than that of a lady escorting four schoolchildren and a guinea pig for a summer holiday?'

'They didn't know about the guinea pig,' Simon said automatically. 'But of course I see now why Mademoiselle was so worried at Boulogne. She really must have been scared of being stopped.'

'Exactly. Then the plan was for him to meet an accomplice in Boulogne and hand over the case of paintings in exchange for a similar case of clothes and perhaps money, and then get away down south. The more different links in the criminal chain the more difficult it is for the police to track them down.'

'So on the train Mademoiselle thought that that was the end of her part of the robbery? She just had to sit back and enjoy herself. No wonder she was so much happier.'

'Precisely, but of course when the accomplice opened the case, he found not the invaluable paintings but . . .'

'My socks!' Simon concluded for him. Although he was so worried about Rose, he couldn't help laughing to think that this great plan should have gone wrong just because of a caseful of old clothes belonging to the Packet family.

'You know the rest,' the Superintendent said. 'The accomplice travelled immediately down south and contacted your mademoiselle, who realized what had happened. Together they went to the house to search for the case. They must have thought you were staying there.'

'Yes, I suppose so. My aunt gave Cynthia's address and I don't expect anybody bothered to mention that we were really staying in the caravans.'

'They found nothing in the house. The next morning they noticed the caravans in the grounds. They realized that you children might be staying in them and decided to go and look for the case.'

'Which they did,' Simon ended sadly. 'And found—Rose.'

* * * *

'So you liked my pictures so much that you hung them up?' the bald man asked Rose. Now that they were approaching the gorge he seemed more confident, more eager to talk and laugh and mock.

'Was that why you came to the caravan?' Rose asked. 'To get your pictures back?'

'We came to visit you, little one,' he replied nastily.

She had been quite right not to like Mademoiselle, Rose reflected. She had been suspicious of her from the beginning. All the same, she had to be fair; Mademoiselle was a wonderful artist.

'They are marvellous pictures,' she said, and even now her voice was enthusiastic when she thought of them. 'Did you paint them all this summer?'

The bald man stared at her in amazement. He seemed stunned. He repeated the question in French and this time the fat man joined in his laughter. As they both laughed the car slowed and for a moment she thought that they might swerve off the road, for they laughed so much that their eyes were quite shut.

It was at that precise moment that she thought she caught a glimpse of a car behind. Just a dark shadow. She wasn't sure—it might have been a trick of the light. If it was a car it must have slowed down for it did not appear again. Perhaps she had imagined it.

XXV

The Chase

'I still don't see why they had to take Rose,' Simon said. 'Unless she tried to stop them taking the paintings.'

'She may have recognized Mademoiselle,' the Superintendent said.

Simon shook his head. He couldn't see any resemblance between the little French woman with her stoop, her red hair, her black hat with the veil, and either of the men they had seen creeping about the house last night.

'They took Rose because they are desperate men,' the Superintendent said grimly.

After that he did not talk. He pressed his foot down hard on the accelerator and the big car almost skimmed the surface of the road, they moved so fast. Simon could sense that he was absolutely determined to catch the men who had taken Rose.

The road climbed more and more steeply. Simon recognized the route they had taken to the gorge only a few days ago. It seemed more like months, he thought.

Suddenly the car stopped with a great jolt. He felt the safety belt take the strain. He looked up at the Superintendent. 'A blue car ahead,' the Superintendent said.

Simon felt a great surge of relief that they might be within sight of Rose.

'I am going to try to catch a glimpse of the people in it,' the Superintendent explained. 'If it is the thieves, then I must keep on their tail, but always out of sight. If it is not, then I mustn't waste time tailing them. It is a pity I have no binoculars in the car.'

'I have,' said Simon, who had the family pair hanging round his neck.

'Excellent. Now I want you to train them very carefully on the road ahead. The minute I see the blue car, I have to slow down, of course, and hope that they don't see me. But in that second, you must try to recognize your sister. All right?'

'All right,' Simon said.

He took the binoculars and trained them on the road ahead, focused them and stared as hard as he could. Not only his eyes strained, but his whole body seemed tensed in readiness.

It all happened in a flash. The glimpse of the blue car, the sudden lurching stop of their own. But in that flash he had seen it—the fair hair, the pink candy stripe dress, just a bit of it, her shoulder perhaps.

'It's her—it's Rose,' he said at once and without a shred of doubt.

The Superintendent nodded, but did not speak.

Simon also sat in silence, marvelling at the way the Superintendent went so fast, but always kept just out of sight of the car in front. He seemed to know exactly what speed the blue car would do. And still the road continued to climb.

*　　*　　*　　*

When she did not see the car again, Rose decided that she must have imagined it. She noticed that the big man, as he drove, kept looking in the mirror to make sure nobody was following and sometimes the bald man looked over his shoulder. They were talking in low voices now and their faces were grim.

As the road grew steeper and steeper, her feeling of dread increased. She could see the deep ravine now and the ribbon of white at the bottom which was the river. The road seemed to cling to the side of the mountain and twisted like a snake ahead of them.

Suddenly she saw the viewing point where they had stood only a few evenings ago. She could see where they had parked the car, the grass they had walked over and the ledge beyond which the rock dropped sheer into the abyss.

As they came up to the viewing point the car swung to the side of the road and stopped. The big man jumped out. The bald man did the same, taking the case of paintings with him. The big man opened the door near Rose and grabbed her arm. She tried to resist, but he pulled her out of the car. She screamed, but even as she did so, realized that it was no use screaming. There was nobody to hear her. There was no life up here in this wild, deserted place. Not even a bird. If it had been any use screaming, they would have gagged her, she thought.

The big man dragged her round the back of the car. On the grass the bald man was standing, holding the case. The big man scowled and shouted at him, pointing to the case and then towards the car. He must be telling him to leave the case in the car. It was only her, not the paintings, that they were going to throw into the gorge. She prepared to fight every inch of the way, to scream and yell and bite.

Then the unbelievable happened. A black car appeared, as if from nowhere, and swung in between them and the ravine. The big man let go of her, the bald man dropped the case and they both dashed to their own car and started off along the road.

For a moment the Superintendent hesitated. Then he said to Simon, 'Get out and look after your sister. I'm following them. Very soon the police car will catch up. Stop it and tell the policeman and the others to wait here with you and Rose. None of you move from here.'

Then he almost pushed Simon out of the car and set off with a roar. He was out of sight round the next corner before Simon could reply.

*　　*　　*　　*

Simon and Rose stood together on the bluff of land above the gorge. Beside them, in the grass, lay the case which had caused all the trouble. From here they could see the road winding its way round the gorge, twisting and turning. They saw the blue car going at an incredible speed round a bend, then it disappeared into a tunnel. They saw the black car follow it round the bend and disappear also. The blue car emerged from the tunnel and shortly afterwards the black car relentlessly followed. The children watched. They could not move. It just did not seem possible that cars should go so fast on such a road.

'They can't keep it up, they can't,' Simon said in a croaking voice for his mouth was dry with excitement. Suddenly the car in front seemed to spin. Like a toy it whirled and span and moved sideways, as a crab might, across the road. It seemed to hesitate for a moment on the edge of the gorge, as if looking down, poised like a diver over the water, and then it slid over the edge, rolling over and over until it disappeared from sight.

The black car stopped. They saw the Superintendent get

out and walk to the edge. For a terrible moment Rose thought he was going to jump over. Nothing seemed impossible today. But he only looked and then walked back to his car.

'He can't turn there,' Simon said. 'He'll have to go back to the junction.' Then suddenly the police car was with them, the nice fat policeman with the cheery red face, and Alain and James and Linda. And Porky. Incredibly, here in this dreadful place was Porky, looking as ordinary as usual.

They all rushed to her, Simon explaining to James and Linda, James explaining to Alain in a mixture of French and English, and Alain explaining to the policeman. It was like one of those games when you whisper messages which get changed as they go from person to person. Only this message was too awful to be altered much, Rose thought.

The policeman took Rose's hands in his, then he kissed her on both cheeks and was much moved. The children looked at each other a bit awkwardly.

'Glad you're all right, Rose,' Simon said. 'We were a bit worried.'

James said, 'Sure you're all right, old thing? They didn't hurt you?'

Linda held Porky out and said, 'Want him?'

Rose took Porky and held him against her shoulder.

'Yes, I'm all right,' she said, stroking the guinea pig. 'Quite all right now.'

Then they all began talking at once.

*   *   *   *

The caravan seemed a bit bare after the pictures had gone, so Rose painted some of her own and put them up instead.

When Pierre and Cynthia came back, they could hardly believe what had happened. They sat talking about it that evening under the pine tree.

'I never did like that Mademoiselle Sourire,' Pierre said. 'From the moment she refused my invitation to picnic and swim, I disliked her.'

They all laughed.

'Goodness, but just think of all those invaluable pictures pinned up in our old caravan,' Cynthia said, and she and Pierre looked at each other with disbelief.

'What do you think will happen to them?' Rose asked.

'They will go back to London and be examined by all kinds of experts and then they'll be put back in their frames and people will go to the exhibition and pay money to look at them.'

'And just think, we had them all to ourselves for days,' James said, 'and hardly bothered to glance at them.'

'I did,' Rose said. She thought of the golden light that streamed from the pictures and of the colours and the wateriness. And she knew she would never forget them, never.

'And what about my socks?' Simon asked.

They all laughed again.

'Fortunately it's too hot for socks,' Cynthia said. 'Because I doubt if you'll see that case again.'

She was wrong. On their last day, as they were finishing breakfast, they looked up to see a tall figure walking across the field with Cynthia and Pierre. It was the Superintendent. He was carrying a black case.

He shook hands with each of them in turn.

'Your clothes, I think?' he said, handing the case to Rose.

'Golly, we thought we'd lost it for good,' Simon said.

The Superintendent smiled. 'Getting it back was the least we could do, after your help in finding the other one,' he said.

He stayed and had breakfast with them and gave them messages from Alain who was now back in Paris with his mother. Then he looked at Rose's paintings in the caravan and seemed to like them very much. He told the children

that the insurance company had offered a reward for finding the pictures and part of it would be divided between
the four of them.

They stared at him in amazement.

'But,' Simon objected, 'we didn't even try to *find* the
pictures. I mean, Mademoiselle *lost* them, but we didn't
really *find* them.'

'Don't be silly, Simon,' Linda said. 'You're always being
so logical about things. We found them in the caravan.'

'Yes, but we didn't look for them, we just happened to
find them.'

'Fortunately the reward was for finding, not looking,'
the Superintendent pointed out.

Then they all began talking about what they would
spend the reward on, until Cynthia told them that if they
didn't hurry and do their packing they would miss the
train.

The Superintendent shook hands again with everybody.
He even took Porky politely by one paw to say good-bye.

'Will it be all right? I mean taking Porky back?' Rose
asked anxiously.

'I promise not to tell the police,' the Superintendent said.

He even wrote a little note to say that Porky was being
allowed to travel, as a reward for the part he had played
in getting back the art treasures.

So Rose did not feel at all anxious about taking him on
to the train. She even held him up to Cynthia and Pierre
as they stood on the platform saying good-bye.

'Promise you'll come next year,' Cynthia said, as the train
moved out.

'We promise,' they replied as with one voice.

The journey back was very uneventful; it seemed to
Rose no time at all before she was back home again.

'I suppose you heard about the paintings?' Simon asked as they sat around the table after tea.

Mother nodded. 'Oh, it was in all the papers,' she said. 'And there's a letter about the reward from the insurance people.'

'Yes, we were told about that.'

'And a special letter from the Gallery for you, Rose,' her father said, getting up and giving it to her.

Rose read it carefully, then she put it down and her face was red with excitement. 'It says I can go to any of their exhibitions and have a special view of the pictures,' she said.

Then she looked down at the box beside her. 'But I don't expect I shall go very often,' she said. 'Because what about Porky?'

'You're mad about that guinea pig,' Simon told her. 'I wouldn't let my stick insects stop me from going to London if I wanted to.'

'Guinea pigs are different,' Rose said firmly, as she got out her painting things and prepared to settle down for the evening.